"Did you feel lonely last night, Emma?"

Simon was gazing at her intently as he went on. "I must confess I was... surprised to wake up and find you in my arms."

"You were having a nightmare. You pulled me into bed with you," Emma answered briefly.

"Phew!" Simon sat down abruptly. "You were lucky to get away unscathed!"

She turned her head to hide her vivid telltale blush. "You've already told me I'm not your type."

"Sometimes a man can judge a little too hastily," he murmured softly.

There was a tense awkward silence. When Emma found the courage to look up again he was studying her closely. "I hope you didn't find the experience too disagreeable—just in case it happens again."

WELCOME TO THE WONDERFUL WORLD OF *Harlequin Romances*

Interesting, informative and entertaining, each Harlequin Romance portrays an appealing and original love story. With a varied array of settings, we may lure you on an African safari, to a quaint Welsh village, or an exotic Riviera location—anywhere and everywhere that adventurous men and women fall in love.

As publishers of Harlequin Romances, we're extremely proud of our books. Since 1949, Harlequin Enterprises has built its publishing reputation on the solid base of quality and originality. Our stories are the most popular paperback romances sold in North America; every month, six new titles are released and sold at nearly every book-selling store in Canada and the United States.

A free catalogue listing all Harlequin Romances can be yours by writing to the

HARLEQUIN READER SERVICE,
(In the U.S.) 1440 South Priest Drive, Tempe, AZ 85281
(In Canada) Stratford, Ontario, Canada N5A 6W2

We sincerely hope you enjoy reading this Harlequin Romance.

Yours truly,

THE PUBLISHERS
Harlequin Romances

The Driftwood Beach

by

SAMANTHA HARVEY

Harlequin Books

TORONTO • LONDON • LOS ANGELES • AMSTERDAM
SYDNEY • HAMBURG • PARIS • STOCKHOLM • ATHENS • TOKYO

Original hardcover edition published in 1981
by Mills & Boon Limited

ISBN 0-373-02481-9

Harlequin edition published June 1982

Printed in U.S.A.

CHAPTER ONE

THE girl on the beach was almost painfully slender. She sat on a high rock at one end of the sand, crouched forward and hugging her knees, her chin resting on pointed kneecaps and the bones of her spine pushing against honey-tanned skin in a clear, curved pressure-line. She wore a flesh-coloured bikini under a transparent cheesecloth blouse, and her hipbones jutted in sharp angles below a tiny waist.

Beneath her the incoming tide swirled pieces of twisted driftwood against the rocks; broken roots and branches swept down by rivers or stolen from the foreshore by encroaching tides. They clattered as the waves rattled them together before sweeping them away for more shaping and smoothing.

There are many such beaches along the east coast of Australia; small curves of white sand and tall cliffs, with the surf breaking and the sky shining down blue and clear through most of the year.

The girl sat watching the driftwood. She seemed not to notice the breaking surf, and she certainly could not see the man who stood watching behind her, half hidden by rocks and shadows in the downcoming dusk.

Apart from the man and the girl the beach was deserted. Earlier that afternoon a change of wind and tide had chopped the waves into white water, and all the surfers had picked up their boards and driven away.

A wave reared high and flung itself against the rock; and as if it were a signal the girl stood up. The man behind her moved slightly, as if to get a clearer view. He stood curiously still, his gaze intent.

He could see her face now; a small elfin face with cleft chin and wide curved mouth adding a surprise dimension that was more enchanting than classically beautiful. Even in repose it was an extraordinary face, with its wide winged brows and fine-planed cheekbones. Her eyes and her hair were coloured alike; deep brown with flecks of glinting gold, the hair a tumbled cloud of curls touching the shoulders.

As the man watched, she stooped and picked up a long full skirt of flowered cotton, pulling it over her head and settling it carefully around waist and hips, as though she dressed to walk away from the beach. But as she climbed down from the rock, another wave swept in and touched her feet. She studied her wet feet dreamily, then began to walk, not away from the sea but towards it. Water swirled over the hem of the long skirt, but she paid it no attention. Slowly, dreamily, she walked into the ocean, wading out carefully.

The sea received her with deceptive gentleness. The first two waves brushed against her softly as she walked waist-deep without faltering; but the next wave was a side-swinger. It scooped her up and dropped her into a trough of green water. Flying spray cascaded down over the flowered skirt until it disappeared under foam.

The girl came up gasping. She raised her arms over her head, as if for protection; then she went under again.

The man on the beach made an impatient sound. As he came out of the shadows, the patchy light showed him to be tall and brown and black-bearded. He wore faded black shorts on a lean, suntanned body with heavily muscled shoulders; and as he sprinted towards the water he kicked off rubber thongs from his feet. They floated among the driftwood.

It took him only seconds to reach the girl, where she floundered helplessly in the enveloping skirt. He shook the waves from his tanned body as though they were of no consequence, and grasped the girl and turned her around to face him.

She fought him furiously, pounding his shoulders until the strength went from her wrists and she sagged against him in surrender. He picked her up roughly, as though it annoyed him to have to take action, and flung her from the undertow into a stretch of quiet water. When she came up spluttering he gathered her under his right arm, balancing the slender body on one hip, and strode out of the water, where he flung her down on to the sand and stood staring at her furiously.

The black beard shone with water-drops and where the dark hair grew back in a curly peak from his wide forehead, two small trickles of water meandered down over his cheeks. Most of his face was obscured by the beard, but the girl could see a long firmly-chiselled nose, green eyes dark-lashed, and a mouth that might have been gracefully curved when relaxed but was now tight in angry disapproval.

For a few minutes they glared at each other, like two antagonists at first encounter; but the girl was shaken, and when she struggled to get to her feet the flowered skirt, heavy and wet, tripped her so that she almost fell.

Silently the man reached out a hand and supported her. She scowled at him.

'Who asked you to interfere? A person can swim——'

'If that was a swim, you weren't doing very well at it, were you? And that's mighty strange gear to wear for your evening paddle. Most people take off their clothes to swim. They don't put on extra stuff.'

'Well, I'm not most people, then. And I d-didn't—I wasn't——'

But she wouldn't look at him. She fumbled with the skirt, wringing moisture from it, anything to avoid his searching scrutiny.

There were blue cold-lines from the pert nose to the wide mouth-corners; and she shivered.

'All right, you'd better get home before you die of cold. Where do you live?'

'I can find the way, thank you.'

She waved a hand vaguely. He strode across to the rocks and picked up a towel.

'Here, drape this around you if you're cold.'

'I'm not c-cold—or shivering. It's just that I—I s-stammer sometimes, that's all.'

The heavy dark brows drew together.

'All right, little Miss Sometimes-stammerer.

Where do you live? I've a Land Rover on top of the cliffs. I'll take you home.'

She tried to hide the fact that his question discomfited her, but the green eyes watched her shrewdly. His thongs had vanished with the driftwood and he wasn't very pleased.

'I c-can get there.'

He still watched her astutely, eyes narrowing as he noted the bones of ankle and instep tight-pressed against the skin, the slender wisp of body in its clinging skirt.

'I know the way, thank you.'

'I'm sure you do,' he drawled. 'But you don't appear to have a car, and you can't walk with that skirt thing clinging around your knees. So you'd better come with me and that'll save us a lot of arguing, won't it? The sooner you get dry the quicker you'll stop shivering.... Now that you've finished thanking me,' he added drily.

She looked at him then, very quietly, flicking his wet face with her enormous eyes, then dropping long eyelashes again, as though she retreated.

'I—I don't have anywhere s-special to go tonight. Actually I—I'm l-looking for somewhere.'

'Are you, now?'

'Yes.'

He wasn't going to let her escape that easily. There was something arrogant in the way he stood assessing her, taking in the body bone-thin under wet clothing, the soft mouth shivering, the secretive veiling of her eyes under long, screening lashes. He asked suddenly, 'How long have you been living on the beach?'

She flung her head back, and this time met his keen perceptive gaze without flinching.

'I haven't. I mean—I s-suppose I should explain.'

The man's expression did not lose its grimness. The girl frowned at her wet blouse and made a half-hearted attempt to rub her arms dry with the towel.

'I've been with my b-brother and his friends. I came up here f-from Melbourne, in Victoria, when my mother died, a few m-months ago. And t-today we had—a disagreement—and they left——'

His eyes swept the beach.

'Taking with them your belongings? I see no personal property.'

'I only h-had a sleeping-bag—and a couple of things——'

'Didn't they leave you anything? How much have you got to live on?'

Silently, she thrust a hand into a pocket of the limp, wet skirt. It came out clutching a sodden wallet which she offered awkwardly. Her soaked hair poured water-drops over it, and she shook it, and undid the clasp.

From under long, spiky lashes her eyes flickered up at him, apologetically.

'T-twenty-five cents,' she said. 'And my d-driving licence, and a couple of other papers.'

'Do you stammer like that all the time, or am I making you nervous?'

She gave him another swift glance from under the long lashes.

'I find you intimidating,' she announced, clearly

and firmly, flushing because his lips curved into a fleeting ghost of a smile. 'You're b-bossy, aren't you?'

'Not always.' He surveyed her thoughtfully. 'What's your name?'

'Emma.'

Gingerly, he unfolded the soaked driving licence and inspected it thoughtfully.

'Emerald Marguerite Wilson. Very fancy. You're eighteen, then, if you hold a driving licence. I wouldn't have believed it. I don't suppose I'd have believed that name, either, if I hadn't seen it in print.'

A flush crept under the blue and white of the cold in her face.

'It was my mother's idea,' she explained. 'My m-mother thought, with a plain name like Wilson, we ought to have something more—more fanciful. M-my brother's name is Godfrey Lancelot—but everybody calls him Willie.'

'Good lord! Not much of a knight in shining armour, is he, to leave his sister stranded with twenty-five cents on the beach!'

Emma's enormous eyes became suddenly secret. She moved her head awkwardly.

'He was v-very angry. I wouldn't do something he wanted me to do.'

She pushed her lips together, eyes defiant. The man pressed no further.

'I see. Well, that leaves only me.' When she made a gesture of denial he added sharply, 'Or the police. They'll soon be after you with a vagrancy charge if you lurk about the Sapphire Coast with twenty-five cents in your pocket and nowhere to go. So come on!'

She towelled herself slowly, refusing to look at him; but when he turned and walked towards the straggling path that led to the clifftop she watched hesitantly. When he failed to look back she pursed her lips, hesitated again, then flung the towel over her shoulder.

He was so confident she'd follow, he didn't even look back as she trailed over his footprints across the white sand, and slowly climbed the cliff. When she reached the grass on top of the cliffs he was sitting in his Land Rover, with the passenger door wide open. Wordlessly she climbed in and sat beside him.

He stroked the wild black beard absently, and as she settled herself he said suddenly, 'I've been thinking, young lady—Emma, is it? Well, what you need is a job; and I just might have one for you.'

When she asked suspiciously, 'What sort of a job?' he laughed. His laughter was derisive.

'Don't be too choosey. You're in what old-time melodrama called "desperate straits", aren't you?'

'I'm not *that* desperate!'

He made a movement of peace with one arm.

'All right, you've made your point. This is perfectly legitimate employment I offer. Wages for effort. I think you could help me, and it looks as if you have need of me at the moment. So after you've had a hot shower and chased pneumonia away, why don't we see if we can work out something to our mutual advantage?' The harsh mouth tilted in a sardonic grin; but his eyes weren't smiling. 'And don't start worrying that you'll be molested. Little beach girls who flounder around in the surf aren't my type.'

When she made no reply, he added softly, 'You're going to have to sleep somewhere tonight, and not on the beach. So it's either the police station or my caravan. You'd better decide forthwith, Emma, so I'll know which direction to drive. In case you feel we haven't been introduced—my name is Simon Charles.'

'Mr Charles——'

'Simon. I may look old enough to be your grandfather, but I'm not.'

'Well, Simon then. I'd want to know more about this job you're offering me. It seems a f-funny sort of—well, odd, isn't it? That it's come up just now, I mean.'

He gave an exasperated sigh.

'All right. I'm heading north from here, and inland . . . to a place where I intend asking some questions, about something that happened five years ago.'

'That's a long time—five years.'

'Yes. I'm following a cold trail, but not necessarily a dead one, Emma. With a bit of luck, I may be able to blow a few sparks into the embers. These enquiries are not official. There are some people I want to talk to, and some other people I'd prefer not to notice me. It occurs to me you might be a big help. A man travelling on his own is a lot more conspicuous than one with a—um—a female attachment.'

The girl sat up straight.

'And you're inviting me to become a f-female attachment?' Her eyes flashed disbelief. 'Y-you've got your nerve, haven't you? I'd rather go and see the police, even if they do decide I'm a v-vagrant. I suppose there are worse things——'

Her voice trailed away uncertainly, before the derisive raising of his eyebrows, the irony of his thin lips smiling . . .

He said drily, 'Spare me your holy indignation. I'm offering you a job, with pay and without strings. You are not about to be ravished in the canvas walls of my annexe; my caravan is not Bluebeard's Castle. Think about it, Emma. Reasonable job, with reasonable pay. You'll have to search pretty hard before you find another this time of year.'

He was right about that; she'd tried a few times in the coastal towns she and her brother's friends had passed through. She wavered; and he nodded grimly.

'Precisely. Can you cook? You'd be a hell of a lot more useful if you can. But if not, I can manage.' He looked at her humorously. 'I haven't poisoned myself so far. I don't suppose I'd poison you.'

'I looked after my mother. Invalid cooking, mostly. But I can cope.'

He nodded. 'Okay then. Let's get back to camp and get you a hot shower. Then we'll discuss how you can help me and I can help you.'

The caravan park was only a short distance away. Neither of them had dried out when the man swung the vehicle expertly between two lines of dark green pittosporum trees, and then slowly around lines of tents and caravans stretching like a small city among the bushland. He stopped outside a concrete shower block, reached behind the seat and pulled out a pair of denim jeans and a shirt patterned with wild red flowers. These he tossed to the girl.

'Both clean,' he announced tersely. 'Neither will be a very good fit, so you'll have to make adjustments. Roll up the legs and sleeves, there's a good girl. And here's a dry towel. Now give me your wallet.'

Emma's eyes widened in childlike surprise. Wrapped in the towel, with sea-water snailing wet trails down neck and face from her thick dark hair, she looked remarkably like a tousled child.

Obediently, one hand wandered towards the pocket where her wallet lay. She pulled it away, sharply.

'No!'

'Yes.' Impatiently he thrust a hand into her pocket and tugged out the wallet.

The bright green eyes glinted. He was smiling with bleak humour.

'My security, in case you're planning to sprint off when you come out of the shower. You'll need your driving licence, won't you, and the other papers. *And* the twenty-five cents.' He grinned. 'You can collect them at the white caravan over there, behind the trees.'

The van he indicated was one of five parked around a power-pole on the ocean edge of the camp; set back a little from the others so that it was half screened by trees, its brown and green striped canvas annexe well camouflaged, and attached like the others to the power-pole by a long electric power lead.

Emma scowled sulkily at his hand with the sodden wallet in it; and nodded.

'I'll be there.'

'I'll expect you.'

Behind the expressionless face, the girl detected a threat. He sat so still, watching her. Like a sea-eagle she remembered watching once, perched on a high tree beside the ocean, still and powerful, ready to spring into instant action if necessary.

She scowled at him again and climbed out of the Land Rover, clutching towel and clothing. She wondered whether he had any dry towels left for himself and hoped he hadn't. Let him stay damp. Let him sit shivering with his suspicions until she chose to come out.

She took her time over the shower, and when it was finished and she had rubbed hair and body dry, she walked haughtily to the white caravan.

Outside one of the other vans, a middle-aged woman collected cups from a picnic table. She paused as Emma approached, watching with bright inquisitive eyes, taking in the slight figure, the ill-fitting jeans, the man's shirt with front ends tied in a loose knot around Emma's tiny waist.

The woman had a sharp but not unpleasant face, hair tinted an unbelievable shade of bronze, and her lips parted slightly as she watched Emma pass, as if she might have spoken.

As the girl went into Simon Charles's caravan the woman put down her teacups and hurried into her own van. She hissed 'George!' and a plump, iron-grey man with a patient face put down his fishing magazine and raised eyebrows enquiringly.

'What now?' he asked.

But Emma saw none of this. She found the man Simon smoothing down the only bed in the caravan. There were two ham sandwiches and a glass of milk on the table, and he waved her towards them.

'Drape your wet gear over the line outside,' he ordered. 'Then eat. After that, you'd better go to bed. Afraid I can't offer you pyjamas, but you can keep that shirt for nightwear. It's a gift.' He grinned, raising one eyebrow mockingly. 'I never did like it anyhow. I don't know why I bought it. Poinsettia flowers aren't my style.'

With a quick movement he stepped between the girl and the wallet that lay on a shelf over the sink. She curled her lips, but said nothing, only picked up her wet clothes and stalked outside.

She was draping the flowered skirt over the line when the older woman approached and stood alongside her.

'You're new, aren't you?' she queried in a sibilant whisper. 'With Mr Charles, I suppose?' She jerked her head in the direction of Simon's van. 'We thought he was alone.' When Emma stayed silent, she added, 'He was alone when he arrived.'

She leaned towards Emma confidentially.

'You're very young, aren't you?'

Emma could see her checking off the separate

items: Emma's youth; the wet blouse and skirt hanging over the line; no rings on Emma's fingers; no shoes on her feet.

'What's your name?'

Emma looked at her in bewilderment.

'Emma,' she admitted.

'Well, Emma, I'm Meriel Harbrow.' She pursed her lips doubtfully. 'If you want anything—in the night—don't be afraid to call out, my dear.'

Emma walked back into the caravan to find Simon regarding her glumly. 'What did that woman want? Meriel whatever-her-name is?'

Emma lifted her face to his great height.

'She said I can call her if—if I w-want anything—in the night,' she told him sweetly. She made a sound then—half sob, half laughter. 'And—and I *will*, too.'

He frowned at her from under lowered dark brows.

'Damn silly woman! All right, you young tiger-cat. You're in no danger from me, in the night or any other time. You needn't lie awake all night ready to scream.'

'I'm n-not a tiger cat!'

He glanced down at her flashing eyes.

'I wouldn't be too sure of that. Now that you've shaken the water off your fur, you could dry out into something very surprising, Emma.'

Without waiting for her reply, he picked up the wallet and strode towards the door. In the doorway he paused and pointed to the bed.

'Yours—all of it,' he drawled sarcastically. 'Safe from mosquitoes, possums and strange men. I'll be sleeping in the annexe. I mention that in case you're planning to slip away before morning. Goodnight, young lady. Pleasant dreams.'

Then he was gone.

After she'd eaten the sandwiches and washed the plate and glass, Emma glanced outside and saw the glow of Simon's cigarette in the evening darkness. Although he had ordered her to bed, he obviously wasn't going to retire so early himself.

Emma looked around the caravan, her eyes widening. Simon Charles travelled in comfort. In addition to the usual caravan stove with two cooking jets, he had a generous oven, a large refrigerator, and although the van carried an LP-gas cylinder outside, it was equipped with a wide range of electrical appliances for when power was available. Emma looked them over with envious eyes. Electric food mixer, juice extractor, frypan, automatic toaster and hot water jug. Curtains and upholstery were all luxurious; and she had eaten from a fine china plate.

No, Simon Charles was not your ordinary camper, prepared to rough it if he had to. He liked the best, and he had surrounded himself with it.

Emma tested the mattress appreciatively. She would sleep in comfort, too. The wide bed occupied the rear of the van, and was designed for restful sleep. Over the luxurious mattress she found a light down-filled covering.

She wondered about Simon, and how he would sleep on the hard floor of the annexe, and spared him no sympathy. She hoped the ground beneath that grass-matting floor was not only hard but uncomfortable. The thought cheered her as she shed everything but Simon's shirt with its scarlet flowers, and crept into bed.

When she heard Meriel Harbrow's voice in the darkness outside a few minutes later, Emma felt better still. The words weren't carrying clearly, but Simon was evidently being subjected to a determined inquisition. His replies were polite but terse.

Emma closed her eyes and allowed herself a small giggle. If there were tears mixed with the laughter it didn't really matter, because at least she'd managed a laugh, her first for several days.

Not far away the bushland surrounding the park ended at the edge of the Pacific Ocean. The splashing of waves on rocks carried clearly from sea-level. It made a rhythmic background to the sounds of the camp. Emma lay listening to the rise and fall of sound, wrapping it around her feelings like a protective blanket.

The conversation outside was still continuing, with Meriel Harbrow's voice low but insistent, as Emma slid quietly, tiredly, and without any intention, into a deep and dreamless sleep.

CHAPTER TWO

THE thin high piping of finches in the melaleuca trees outside the caravan woke Emma next morning. That, and the early morning sounds of the camp stirring. Fishing rods and sinkers rattled, boat-trailers clanked, early morning swimmers set out in muffled bursts of conversation.

Emma rolled over, stretched, then sat up in a surge of alarm. After working out where she was, and why, she climbed slowly out of bed and dressed. To her surprise Simon had already collected her dried skirt and blouse from the clothes line. They lay neatly folded on the padded bench beside the caravan table.

Emma was cooking breakfast when Simon came back from a morning swim. He took in the boiling jug, the set table, and grinned.

'Decided to accept the job, have you?'

Emma watched sceptically as he brushed the wild black hair into some kind of order.

'It all depends. What are you up to? Something illegal?'

His voice was soft and cold.

'I've told you all you need to know, so don't start snooping, Emma. I'm searching for somebody—someone who can tell me something I want to know. If I get answers to my questions I'll recover more than I could spend paying you housekeeping money in a hundred years. Your presence will help me, so don't be bashful about accepting your—er—just reward. I'm not a poor man. You're my cover—that innocent face of yours is going to disarm suspicion while I do what I have to do.'

'You mean, I'm to be your f-female attachment?'

He laughed then, and the laughter for the first time touched the green eyes and set them twinkling.

'Whatever you prefer to be called. Red herring, smoke screen, take your choice. Your youthful charm,' he grinned mockingly, 'would disarm the most suspicious members of the human race.' He turned back from the mirror and faced her squarely. 'What do you say, Emma? Will you come with me, or do you prefer life on the beaches? Of course, you could be lucky if you stay, you might be adopted by a rich surfer; but from what I've seen, I gather rich surfers aren't exactly plentiful.'

Emma put the plate of eggs and bacon in front of him as he sat at the table. 'I must be crazy, but I accept.' She admitted shamefacedly, 'I can't think of anything else to do, anyway. How would I earn my money? Wash your clothes, and cook, and clean the caravan. It doesn't sound like hard work. What shall I do today?'

'We're going shopping. First, for food supplies. The cupboards aren't empty, but they're not exactly full, either. Also, you need a few clothes. Eventually, we'll be leaving the beach and travelling inland, so you'll need to be properly attired. And thirdly,' he hesitated, looking at her with rueful eyes across the table, 'we're going to buy you an engagement ring.'

'A what!'

'Oh, don't panic. Just another bit of camouflage. I'd forgotten the Meriel Harbrows of this world. That woman,' he turned moodily to his breakfast, 'I'll bet there's one like her to every square foot in purgatory. Scandalmongering old witch!' He fingered the mass of springy black hair on his chin. 'She doesn't trust bearded men—she said so. And I'm not shaving it off for her or anybody else. I've just spent weeks growing it.'

Emma said innocently, 'She's looking after my interests. And don't bother about the ring. I can manage my own affairs, thank you.'

'Emma, I'm not going to be accused of corrupting your innocence. We're going in to Jerinda, anyway. You can't cook if you've nothing to put in the pot, so hurry up and we'll get moving. I'll *lend* you the ring; you can return it when our little stint is over if it makes you feel better.'

The streets of Jerinda were crowded with holiday shoppers. Simon and Emma bought meat first, and stowed it in the small portable freezer. Then groceries.

'Now, the ring.'

Emma looked down at her fingers, spreading them out thoughtfully. 'I've never worn a ring. I don't like them much. Do I have to?'

He raised both eyebrows this time, and pushed her towards the footpath while he stacked the last parcel. 'We'll try and find one you can bear.'

There was only one small jeweller's shop in

Jerinda, and when Simon told the owner what they were looking for he beamed and said genially, 'Engagement ring, is it? Diamonds, of course.'

And Simon's face went cold and hard as he snapped, 'No. Anything but diamonds.'

The salesman gave him a swift astonished glance and put back the small tray of rings he was lifting out of his safe. He brought out another one and Simon murmured, 'Emeralds?' lifting one eyebrow in a quizzical way that Emma realised was his method of half-apologising because he wasn't offering her diamonds. But Emma shook her head: he didn't want diamonds, she wouldn't accept emeralds.

They looked over several trays, while Emma protested and shook her head and mumbled, 'I don't care. Really I don't. Do I have to wear one?'

The jeweller tried nobly to hide his amazement. He suggested doubtfully, 'Perhaps you'd care for a pearl?' and Emma was about to shake her head yet again when he brought the pearl ring from the back of his safe, and Emma drew a deep breath of delight.

One pearl, creamy and pure and almost perfectly round, set in delicate filigree loops of gold. Simon slid it on to her finger and it sat there like a flower, fitting perfectly. Her protests died, and she was sent outside while Simon paid for the jewel.

Afterwards, when he joined her on the footpath, Emma moved her hand to catch the gleaming of her ring. She said hesitantly, 'It must have cost the earth. A dress ring would have done.'

He murmured absently, 'Consider it a bonus,

Emma, for work you'll do very well, I'm sure,' and she knew the subject was closed.

'Now, some clothes.'

When she protested he quietened her tersely.

'I'm not carting around a bedraggled waif. I'm travelling with a bright, seductive lady-friend. That's you.'

She didn't like the way he said it. The sardonic smile she was beginning to dislike twisted his mouth once more. She glared at him resentfully.

'Serves you right if I buy the shop out!'

But she knew she wouldn't. She didn't want to be indebted to this man any more than she had to be. Something about him made her uneasy; a feeling of hidden potential that disturbed her. He spoke pleasantly enough most of the time, but there were undercurrents suggesting unpredictable behaviour if he were deeply stirred.

Emma had met other people like that, they always made her feel cautious. She wasn't afraid of Simon, not in a girl-man way. But there were signs of frightening energy and power. This was a man who would sweep aside anyone who got in his way, and she didn't like being swept aside, and she didn't like feeling threatened.

She certainly wasn't afraid of being seduced. But she objected to being treated as if her wishes didn't matter. She liked to make her own decisions.

Yet here was this man with the cold hard mouth and bitter green eyes making all her decisions for her, as if she were a nonentity, a helpless juvenile.

So she searched the racks of skirts and jeans and dresses, and chose sparingly. One pair of jeans, another brightly-coloured cotton skirt, long enough to touch her ankles, and several bright tops. A yellow simulated silk dress since Simon had specified 'something decent'; and a long-sleeved shirt because he insisted that inland the sun and wind were harsher and stronger, without the cool sea breezes she was used to. A parka for cold nights, briefs and bra and a shortie nightdress. She couldn't sleep for ever in Simon's shirt, though she would make it do until they got wherever they were going. A pair of strappy sandals, and heavier boots for walking. Thongs, and a hat, because he insisted.

'I never wear hats.'

'You will,' he announced, standing by while she purchased a shady woven straw that tied under her chin with a cord, which she hated. But he said, 'Where we're going, you might not always be able to hang on to your hat,' and she shrugged and said maliciously, 'Sounds like paradise, this place we're going to.'

But he didn't enlighten her. He might not have been prepared to provoke Meriel Harbrow, but he certainly didn't mind tantalising Emma. Perhaps he didn't trust her. The thought made her uneasy. Not that she trusted him entirely.

Looking at those self-assured green eyes she felt antagonism stir, as though she had been summoned to combat. But she could hide her feelings ... Juvenile Simon might think her, but she wasn't nearly as juvenile as he expected.

He checked everything she had bought, then he said, 'Well, you're prepared for anything now, aren't you?' and she widened her gold-brown eyes and gave him a secret, reserved little smile.

After he had stowed away her parcels he sent her away to buy newspapers and fruit; and when she came back to the vehicle he was missing. Emma was astonished at the chill of fear that assailed her because he was not there.

'Ridiculous,' she thought. 'He hasn't deserted me. He wouldn't leave the Land Rover.'

He was a long time away. Emma stood on the sunlit footpath, brown paper bags of fruit cradled in folded newspapers, studying the faces of bustling strangers, not one of whom spared her a glance. She was relieved, almost joyful, to see Simon at last threading his way through the holidaymakers towards her.

He carried a cardboard box and a plastic carry-bag. 'Some things you probably forgot,' he explained. 'Evening dress. I saw it in a window, and it looked the right size.' He gave her a slight, lopsided grin. 'Here's hoping, anyway. If it's too large we'll have to fatten you up. You could do with a bit of it. And silver sandals and a—what-to-you-call-it—a shawl.'

'You're spending an awful lot of money.' She took the plastic bag hanging between his fingers. 'Tell me, just what do you hope to get out of all this?'

'I'll get my money's worth.'

'Don't be too sure.'

He swung around, then, standing directly in her path and lowering down at her out of those cold green eyes, so that she took an apprehensive half-step backwards. Then she collected her dignity and tilted her face upwards with small jaw firm-set, while her eyes flashed; and he half laughed as he swung the cardboard box between them.

'Hey! Whoa!'

'I didn't ask you to buy any of this.'

'No, you didn't. But if you think I want to make myself conspicuous dragging you around in tatters, you're mistaken. I have a role for you to play, Emma, and I'm dressing you for it. Okay?'

She hesitated, and he thrust the box at her impatiently. 'Here! Earn your money and carry it yourself. And you can leave everything behind when you and I part company, if you want to, though I don't know what I'd do with them. Buy yourself anything else you want with your wages.'

'I get wages, too?'

'You'll earn what you get. Keep the dust out of the caravan, and the good food coming; beds made and dishes washed.'

But as he opened the door of the Land Rover and took the parcels from her he paused a moment and looked down at Emma where she stood, and she saw that his mouth was a thin, grim line and his eyes like bitter glass.

'We have work to do, Emma—serious work. Don't start making waves about trifles, for heaven's sake.'

But the ruthless mood had evaporated by the time he packed away the fruit and newspapers and the cardboard box. He leaned back against the seat, relaxed, his hands with their long brown fingers resting on the steering wheel. He watched her silently, his eyes softened with secret smiling.

She said crossly, 'Whatever's making you laugh, you'd better make up your mind whether you're going to tell me or not. It's no good just sitting there laughing.'

He turned quickly and looked at her again, this time with surprise.

'You know, Emma,' he offered finally, 'I don't think you're going to be as amenable as I expected. That remark sounded waspish.'

Emma looked at him from under lowering brows.

'Of course I'm not amenable,' she snapped. 'You should have asked my brother. He'd tell you.'

'Would he now?' He surveyed her thoughtfully. 'Well, I'll put you out of your misery, Emma, before you start nagging.' His lips twisted in the familiar sardonic smile that made her feel so uneasy. 'I've been to see a marriage celebrant.'

Her lips parted.

'A what?'

'Don't blow a gasket! I thought it advisable, in case anybody is dogging our movements. Mrs Harbrow, for instance. She's a born busybody, that one, quite likely to accuse me of abduction. It's easily disproved but I don't want to take the time or trouble to do it. I don't want attention drawn to myself, so we'll avoid any problems, real or imaginary. So there we are ... You can tell that Harbrow woman tomorrow, or next time she comes up with any more of her acid comments, that we've registered our notice of intended marriage.'

'Our what?'

'Notice of intended marriage. Because of your tender age, my dear Emma, you have to come with me and sign it. After which you wait a month and a day, before you can become my legal happily wedded wife.'

'I wouldn't marry you——'

'The feeling is mutual. Just come with me, like a good girl, and sign the document. And if we don't turn up in a month and a day—which we won't—the good marriage celebrant will, no doubt, find a place for it among his incompleted transactions, and no one will worry. Do you have a birth certificate?'

'Yes. In the wallet. I had to get it for my driving licence.'

'Give it to me, like a good girl, and we'll be on our way.'

Reluctantly, Emma did as she was told. She didn't like any of it. She didn't like the curiously bland expression on the face of the marriage celebrant as he observed her total lack of bridal flutters.

Afterwards, she looked at the pearl ring and it no longer seemed quite as magical as it had when Simon placed it on her finger. She saw it now for what it was—a symbol of commitment, even if only a ghostly, fleeting one. And she was far too young to make any kind of commitment, transitory or permanent. It would be a relief when she could take the ring off, and walk away from the caravan, and never see the tall dark man with the bitter mouth again. She found herself wishing desperately that she had never met Meriel Harbrow, or Simon, either.

She said nothing as she sat waiting for Simon to start the four-wheel-drive. She felt totally drained; the enormity of what was happening to her standing out suddenly sharp and clear. Here she was with a stranger, a man she hadn't even met yesterday morning, wearing his ring, recording her intention to marry a person she had no intention of marrying, with no idea where she would be next week or even tomorrow. And there was no one she could turn to for support.

She was, she told herself drearily, worse off than the bits of driftwood she'd watched on the beach. At least they had each other to jostle against, while she had nothing and nobody . . . unless she counted Simon. And she certainly didn't yet know enough about the man sitting so quietly next to her to be certain whether he could be counted or not.

The man glanced at her obliquely as he inserted the key in the ignition; at her hands stiffly folded in her lap with the ring uppermost, as though she were overwhelmingly aware of its weight on her finger.

He said suddenly, 'Tell you what, Emma; after all this junketing around why don't we get a counter lunch at the hotel? I'll drive back to the camp and stow the food in the van while you hold a table. By the time the meal is ready, I'll be back.'

He made her drink a glass of cold beer before their huge plates of curried prawns, and another afterwards. Then he said, 'There's a small wild life park along the Princes Highway I want to see. A friend of mine owns it. You don't mind being away for the afternoon, do you?'

Emma shook her head and followed him meekly, and as they drove along the highway the sun beamed in through glass windows and either the meal or the cold beer, or both, had wrought some sort of change in Emma, because she found herself relaxing, the clouds of foreboding lifted.

Simon's friend was a square-faced, square-bodied man with an obvious love for the birds and animals in his care. He took Simon and Emma through enclosures where peacocks and guinea-fowl and geese scratched among grasses in the sun, and into paddocks where wallabies and kangaroos loped up sniffing for attention.

They visited the 'joey' nursery, a collection of baby kangaroos rescued from the pouches of dead mothers who had wandered from the forest on to the highway and been killed by traffic.

Curled in 'substitute pouches' of woollen sweaters or hessian bags, they peered out from soft furry faces topped with large pointed ears.

'We get a constant supply,' the guide said sadly. 'Rescuers bring them here and we feed them on eggs and milk until they're old enough to join the older animals out on the grass.' He smiled at Emma cheerfully, 'Here—like to hold one?'

So Emma found herself clutching a furry, long-legged joey wrapped in a woollen jumper. She sat on the wooden nursery floor, soothing him to sleep with gentle hands while Simon and his friend looked through the aviaries of bright Australian birds.

When they came back Emma sat with her back propped against the wall, long lashes drooping over her tired eyes, while her fingers stroked drowsily the soft fur of the sleeping joey.

The long, lean man stood looking down at her, a smile softening the severity of his usual sombre expression. Then he leaned down and said curtly, 'Time to go, Emma,' and Emma handed over the tiny animal and followed Simon meekly to the car park.

She watched with interest the streams and forests on either side of the highway as they drove back. She felt better now, better than she had felt for days. Thinking back, she still wasn't sure what she had intended when she walked into the surf. She didn't suppose, now, that she would ever be certain.

She knew Simon suspected she'd gone on deliberately, not caring whether she ever came out. But she didn't recall ever making any such decision. She only recollected sitting high on the rock, watching the driftwood, listening to the mournful slither of water over wet sand.

She'd been almost numb, unable to accept that her life for the second time in a few months had suddenly fallen to pieces, until she didn't know which way was tomorrow nor what had happened to yesterday.

Then she had clambered down from the rock and her feet had taken her to the water's edge, as though the whole thing were something she was dreaming; and she'd gone along with the dream, walking over damp sand into the ocean, wondering where it would take her. But she couldn't expect Simon to understand that.

How could she explain to him that she didn't know what she was doing? That even now she felt as if she were being steadily carried away by a wave of events that was stronger than she would ever be. She wasn't really making decisions; they were all being made for her.

She hoped she knew what she was doing, but she certainly wasn't sure what it was leading to.

She would cook for Simon and keep the caravan clean, and supply him with a cover of innocence for whatever he was up to . . . wherever he was going . . .

Oh, heavens! Suppose he was involved in something criminal . . . like drug-selling, or stealing . . .

She stole a quick look at his grim profile as he swung the Land Rover around the shower block towards the caravan. No, it wouldn't be anything criminal. Emma didn't know why she was so sure of it. It had something to do with the fact that Simon carried with him an aura of integrity, an air of judging, not of being judged. He might be arrogant and domineering, even inconsiderate, but never corrupt. And he had given her the ring . . .

She glanced down at it surreptitiously, hoping Simon wouldn't notice, watching the delicate pearl gleaming under its satin skin as though a heart pulsed deep inside . . .

She took her attention from the pearl ring as Simon swung the vehicle in a deft semi-circle; and there was the caravan and the striped annexe, bright in the sunlight, and alongside it, parked between the Harbrows' van and Simon's, a white car with official insignia on its door, two police officers sitting waiting, calmly and patiently, as though they had forever, and were not in any hurry to go away at all.

The bitter betrayal of it shook Emma so hard that she came out of her dreaming and raised two hands with outspread fingers and pressed them against her face; so there were only her stricken eyes for Simon to see when he turned to her.

'You told them!' she whispered, accusing him; and he bent low to hear, shaking his head.

'No.'

He parked his vehicle beside the caravan, taking his time about it and watching her.

She sat rocking quietly in the seat beside him, with her eyes shut tightly now, the fingers of both hands pressed against her lips to stop them trembling.

Simon turned off the ignition and put a hand gently on her arm. 'No,' he said again, 'I didn't, Emma. I've told nobody.'

Then he helped her down on to the grass and put his arm around her, supporting her as they walked towards the policemen who were slowly, calmly, alighting from their car. Simon spoke to the senior officer.

'What do you want?'

'May we come inside, sir?'

There was nobody visible in the Harbrows' caravan. No curtain flickered at the windows, but even in her horror Emma had the prickling feeling of being under surveillance.

She allowed Simon to usher her into the caravan, and they all sat around the table uncomfortably. The police officers were stoical. They glanced quickly from Simon to Emma, then the sergeant pulled out his notebook and asked briskly, 'Emerald Marguerite Wilson?'

'Yes,' Emma snapped, 'of course I am. You know I am.' She noticed Simon sat between her and the door, and wondered if it had been deliberate, in case she ran away. No doubt he'd reached the conclusion that she was the sort of person who fled from danger. But her knees had turned to jelly and she was glad to be sitting down. Her last spurt of defiance had vanished with her testy reply to the sergeant.

Simon asked quietly, 'What brings you here, sergeant?'

'Acting upon certain information,' he coughed. 'Ah—we have received an enquiry——'

'If you're talking about that Harbrow woman and her unspeakable suspicions—Emma is eighteen.'

'I know that, sir.' Was there a glimmer of unease behind that impassive face as he glanced at Simon? 'There's no suggestion——'

'All right, then. What is the suggestion?'

The sergeant hesitated. He might have looked impassive, but he wasn't enjoying his task. The scared girl and the competent man made an appealing if unusual pair. He wished he could leave them alone, but he couldn't. 'Duty,' he thought, and sighed heavily.

'My colleagues in Haenville, a small town farther north,' he announced formally, 'have intercepted a car during the process of roadworthy checks. In that vehicle they discovered certain items of stolen property. A considerable amount, I may say.'

'Whole boot-full. Not to mention the glove-box,' the young constable remarked, not without relish. His senior gave him a silencing look, and he coughed apologetically and lapsed into silence.

'The occupants of this car—five young people—have admitted stealing the property in and around this district. They informed the investigating officers that Miss Wilson here—Miss Emerald Wilson—was party to the thefts.'

Emma jerked upright, face flushed.

'It isn't true!'

'Well, miss, the police at Haenville have statements from the young people involved. One of them, a Mr Godfrey Wilson, is I understand your brother.'

Emma said, her voice incredulous, 'You mean, *he* told you I stole things?'

Simon intercepted quickly, 'Emma!' and his voice was cold and hard and final. Emma glanced at him sharply, then hunched her shoulders.

He asked, 'When are these thefts supposed to have taken place, sergeant?'

'During the past few days, sir. They're all recent thefts, I understand, according to local shopkeepers.'

'That settles it, then. Emma—Miss Wilson—has been with me for two weeks.'

'Really, sir?'

They didn't believe it, either of them. The young constable let his attention flicker from Emma to Simon. The sergeant privately felt a flash of relief. He never did like these things involving silly young girls who felt life should be easier than it was.

He said hopefully, 'With you, sir? You'll swear to that, of course. You may have to. May I ask where, sir?'

'Along the coast, farther south. And around here. We arrived at this park yesterday morning—at least I did. Emma wanted to swim at a small beach not far from here, so I picked her up after I'd settled in.'

'And you never were with your brother and his friends, miss?'

Simon said quickly, 'Of course she was. Until we met, as I told you, a couple of weeks ago. Then Emma and I decided to—er—join forces. The young folk were upset by her decision. They're probably trying to get their own back. So you have my word against the allegations of a number of dubious—I might say extremely unreliable—young people, who most likely are trying to include Emma in the mess because they were annoyed when she left them.'

'You'll swear to that in court, sir?'

Simon remained implacable. 'Naturally. Oh—and you might care to visit the local marriage celebrant, where we've lodged our notice of intention to get married. I'd hardly,' he added suavely, 'be arranging to marry a girl I'd only met yesterday. Would I?'

The sergeant was relieved, although careful not

to show it. He said blandly, 'And you won't object to giving us a statement?'

Emma sat numbly while Simon dictated his statement, easing her gently out of the trap.

When the police had gone, Emma forced her shaking knees to help her move from the table. She glowered at Simon, standing in the doorway.

'P-perjury!' she accused.

Simon's eyes darkened until the green was almost black. 'Yes,' he agreed sardonically. 'Aren't you lucky?'

She sagged, and he might have supported her, but she grasped the table edge and eased herself gently back into the seat. Her face was white and empty.

'Thank you,' she said formally. 'It was very kind of you—t-to save me.'

And he bent his head in mock courtesy.

'Now,' he ordered, 'tell me, have I got myself involved with a juvenile delinquent, or a fully-fledged shoplifter? Where do you come from, Emma, and what have you been doing? You understand I have to know, don't you?'

She filled her lungs, taking a deep long breath as though she filled herself with courage. Haltingly, she told him what there was to tell, although, as she told it, in small ragged sentences, it wasn't much. How, after she had left high school, she had taken care of her mother.

'My father—he didn't stay with us.' Her soft lips twisted bitterly when she confessed that. 'He f-found somebody else, and left my mother to look after us. Then he got killed in a car smash, we heard. He'd been gone a long time. It didn't seem to matter when he died . . .'

Her mother had considered him dead when he left them. Emma remembered that clearly. Their mother mourning, as if death had taken him away, and not the fancy for another woman.

Then when Willie, her brother, had turned his back on school and gone with his friends to travel the beaches, their mother had lost heart altogether. She had lost all interest in life and living, and become a permanent invalid, hopeless and despairing.

Once, Emma remembered, just before she died there had seemed to glow a fleeting strength in her, so that she made some effort to grow strong and leave the bed she clung to. That had made it all the harder one morning when Emma went into her bedroom and she lay fast asleep, yet not asleep, as though her exhausted heart had stopped beating from sheer weariness.

After her mother's death Emma left the small rented room in Melbourne and travelled by coach to the small seaside town where her brother lived with his friends. Willie's friends, the two boys and two girls he had travelled with, had welcomed her. She remembered the change, and how wonderful it had been to belong in a house where there was continual laughter and singing and chattering.

At first they had hidden their stealing from her. When they left one small town and drove north to the next, in an ancient car owned by one of the boys, Emma had believed it was because they had tired of the old place and wanted change of scene.

When they went into hotels along the way, because she wasn't used to drinking she waited outside, or explored the beaches, then drove them wherever they wanted to go. If their singing grew a little slurred it didn't matter. They were happy, and the warmth of their friendship was something Emma had only dreamed of while she took care of her mother. If they lived a little richly for youngsters drawing only unemployment cheques, Emma failed at first to notice. When she did realise what they were doing, from scraps of conversation, they were astonished by her reaction.

'We're not hurting anybody,' they'd protested. They played it like a game, breezing in and out of shops, and whistling their way through parking lots, augmenting their slender incomes with shop-lifting and petty thefts. 'Collecting', they called it. Not robbery, not even petty theft. Certainly not crime. They did it laughingly, stealing fruit, wallets, tins of food, clothing, whatever they fancied.

'All probably insured,' they assured her lightly. 'We're merely relieving people of excess goods.'

They lived peacefully, quite unperturbed by what they were doing. Emma realised it was a way of life and that she couldn't live with it and they were not going to change. So she'd left them . . . with anguish, and the realisation that there would be no more laughter for her, and she had nowhere to go.

Her brother had been at first angry, then disgusted. He and his friends had driven away in their old, battered car, leaving her with nothing.

'A moralising prude', Willie had called her, but she didn't tell Simon that. Willie was only a few years older than she was, but he'd been on the beaches since he was fifteen, and she felt young and awkward and inadequate because she couldn't stay with him. The weeks of warmth and careless friendship and acceptance were all she had ever had of life that was really enjoyable . . . and she'd had to turn her back on all of it.

Which was why she had been sitting on the rock listening to driftwood clattering, feeling a hundred years old and at the same time as if she had just come into the world after a long and difficult birth.

She gave Simon the bare outlines, but Simon's shrewd eyes told her that he knew it all. Whatever she had been, however she had felt, Simon would know it.

He sat there, coolly assessing the things she told him, adding her up, leaning his strong brown hands on the table. Always in control. Sitting there, she thought desperately, as if he'd never done anything wrong in his life. She wanted to ask, didn't you ever make any mistakes? But she knew she wouldn't.

She sat twisting her hands together, and all the loveliness and pleasure had gone out of the beautiful ring Simon had bought her. She felt as if she'd stolen it.

He said finally, 'We'd better leave here as soon as we can. Tomorrow, I think.' He stopped her protest with a gesture. 'The farther we get away from here the better. I'll let the good sergeant know where we're going and tell him we'll probably be back in a month to visit our friend the—er—

marriage celebrant. That'll give us some time. I scent Meriel Harbrow in this somewhere. How else would the police find you were with me?

Emma's eyes were enormous in her pinched white face.

'You still want me to stay with you?'

'Of course I want you. That's what you were hired for, isn't it?'

He stood up abruptly.

'Forget it,' he commanded. 'It's as good as over. I don't think we'll hear any more from the police, or from your brother.' A wintry smile thinned the hard lips. 'I'm quite prepared to continue trusting you with the housekeeping money. I accept your word that you didn't steal.' This time the smile was a little gentler. 'I don't think you're smart enough, anyway, to go tripping around collecting other people's belongings. You don't have the proper face for crime. You'd look guilty as hell.'

Emma's breath was a long wavering sigh that died in her throat.

'Why would he tell them that?' she asked. 'Willie, I mean. He's my brother.'

'Angry, perhaps? Suspecting you'd reported him and his mates, in your excess of moral indignation. He may have believed that when his car was pulled up.'

'No.' Emma's voice was ragged, stiff with pain. 'He's my b-brother,' she repeated in a small, numb voice. Looking down at her clasped hands, feeling more bereft than she had been the morning her mother died. Determinedly she blinked back tears, unable to lift her eyes to Simon's.

Simon paused in the caravan doorway, bending his head slightly to avoid the framework. His eyes were cynical.

'Lesson for the week, Emma,' he told her. 'You might as well face it. The behaviour of one's brother is not always—er—brotherly.'

She thought he'd gone. The door clicked and the coloured plastic ribbons over the annexe entrance rustled. Then they fluttered again, the door opened, and Simon was back.

He looked at her, across the hands she pressed helplessly again over her mouth and cheeks to hold back tears.

'Don't forget dinner,' he demanded. He nodded curtly at the refrigerator. 'Steak and tomatoes, I think. And you might slice some onions. Is there any icecream left?'

She unclasped her hands and stared at him.

'Yes, there is ice-c-cream.'

'Hop to it, then. We'll eat as soon as we can.' He waited while she stumbled from the table and opened the refrigerator before he left. Emma furiously pulled steak from the meat compartment. She reached into the vegetable rack and slapped onions and tomatoes on to the workbench. How callous could you get? Worrying about food in the middle of emotional disaster. Her world in ruins, and he wanted steak and onions! Pride shattered, heart aching with tears, and that was all the sympathy he could offer—that she'd better get busy with the dinner because he was hungry.

It was only as she plugged in the electric frypan that Emma realised how the tall man, by his lack of tact and sympathy, was enabling her to put the pieces of her lost composure together. She couldn't possibly collapse now, not in the act of frying steak and onions. She managed a small, doleful giggle through her veil of tears.

By the time Simon came back to the caravan, she had managed at least the outward appearance of calm. He'd changed into black cotton jeans and a turquoise shirt that threw strange lights on to his eyes, turning them opalescent instead of the habitual clear green. Though they softened his expression, they still kept his secrets very well. His face remained impassive as he stared down at her.

Emma looked at him guiltily. She had brought down the police around his head, and that was something he wouldn't like at all. But his eyes remained inscrutable.

Simon wasn't tailor-made to fit a caravan. His height, and the broad muscular shoulders under the loose shirt, took up most of the available space between Emma and the table.

The smell of frying steak and onions wafted through the caravan and he sniffed it appreciatively. He lingered a few moments as though he might have something more to say. Then he got out of her way, and she saw him relaxing on a lounger outside.

When Meriel Harbrow came out of her own caravan, Simon carefully rearranged the newspaper he was reading, spreading it over his face and lying back in simulated sleep.

Even so, lying back relaxed in pretended slumber, he knew how to send out a force-field of intimidation that kept intruders away. He was doing it now, to Meriel Harbrow, as Emma watched. The woman glanced, hovered, and then retreated into her own caravan.

CHAPTER THREE

EMMA faced the approaching evening with dread. She knew it would be long and dreary and she didn't know what to do with it. It was no use talking any more to Simon; all the talking had been drained out of her. She felt numbed with shock and beneath the numbness she was aware of anger and despair simmering, waiting to take over. Yet there was no part of it she could share with anybody.

Whatever Simon had to say it would be disapproving, that was for sure. Desperately, Emma sought for a way to dodge his probing questions, finding it at last in the crossword puzzle from the newspaper when he discarded it.

It wasn't a difficult puzzle, but she managed carefully not to fill it in too fast, so that she could pore over it until bedtime.

Last night she had drifted to sleep listening to the splash of surf on the rocks below. Tonight she could not sleep at all. After Simon had said a bleak goodnight she crept under the sheet and tossed and turned until the caravan clock, touched by a beam of light through the open window, told her it was two o'clock in the morning.

She crept to the doorway and listened to Simon's regular breathing. He was fast asleep. Emma opened the curtains wide enough to see what she was doing. She felt in the wardrobe for her flowered skirt and the cheesecloth blouse she had been wearing when Simon rescued her; and when she was dressed she opened the drawer and took five dollars from the wages he had given her. The rest she left in the drawer. The camp was silent. Carefully, Emma slipped the pearl ring from her finger and placed it on a shelf over the stainless-steel draining board where Simon would find it in the morning.

Slowly and stealthily she eased open the door, tiptoed across the annexe, and let herself out, walking quickly down the camp exit road, across bands of silver light and dark caravan shadows, until she came to the gates and the access roadway.

Along the roadside she flitted silently under trees, her feet making only small brushing noises in the dust and dry leaves. Except for distant surf the night was almost totally silent. Trees twisted in grotesque dark splashes; an occasional bird or possum rustled. That was all.

Emma didn't look behind her. She hadn't noticed the curtains fluttering in the Harbrows' caravan as she fled . . . It wouldn't have mattered if she had. She was completely turned off by the whole human race, and that most certainly included Meriel Harbrow. She hated them all.

But Meriel Harbrow was worrying. 'That girl,' she whispered, and her voice was troubled, 'she's gone, George—done a midnight flit. And the man hasn't followed her!'

George Harbrow was accustomed to his wife's dramatics. 'Go back to sleep,' he grunted. 'She's a grown young woman, isn't she? She knows what she's doing.'

But Meriel Harbrow lay a long time staring out into the night. It wasn't her affair. Surely she should feel free to ignore it . . . But Emma had stirred her protective instincts, and for all her acid tongue and suspicious nature, she was not without compassion. She lay staring at Simon's caravan, willing him to wake and follow the girl, until at last her aching elbow forced her to let the curtain drop.

Simon had not followed Emma. Everything around the caravans remained still and silent. Meriel did not know whether to be relieved or sorry. She had wanted desperately to rescue the slip of a girl from the bearded man with the arrogant manner. Her first reaction when she had seen Emma with Simon had been righteous indignation, soon to be swamped—though not entirely—by powerful curiosity. How and where did a man like that pick up a little waif with those enormous haunted eyes and the slender child's body and the air of needing love and protection?

Now she wasn't so sure. The protection of a strong man might be preferable to being entirely defenceless, as Emma would be now.

Possibly Meriel Harbrow would have been even more worried had she seen Emma stumbling along the roadside, in and out of shadows. Once a passing young motorist stopped to offer her a lift. He pulled up with brakes squealing and thrust his head out of the window, shouting, 'Hey! What's a good-looking chick like you doing out on her own?'

When Emma gave no answer he revved up the motor. 'Enjoy your walk, then, love,' he shouted sarcastically after her disappearing figure.

Although she paid him no attention the boy's overtures penetrated Emma's misery. She turned away from the roadside into the bushland along the foreshore, walking because the track was there, yet too miserable and defeated to wonder where she was going.

When her feet lost their strength she found herself on the small grass picnic area at the top of the cliffs, overlooking the beach where Simon had found her. She had not set out to walk there, yet somehow her weary body had found its way. There were picnic tables and benches near the beach track; Emma sat on a bench and cupped her chin in her hands, staring down at the shadowed rocks and the curve of sand with the waves licking its tideline.

Her thoughts were not coherent. All she knew with certainty was that she seemed, most unfairly, to have far more than her share of troubles; and she wasn't sure she could cope much longer.

She stared at the waves, then at last put her weary head on her folded arms and slept.

When dawn came and a few rabbits ventured out to sniff the grasses, Emma uncurled herself from the bench slowly, letting the circulation seep painfully back into stiff limbs.

She stood on the grass, turning her head slowly as if she might have searched for some kind of direction. Then she turned slowly and walked back the way she had come.

Leg muscles ached and protested, her head felt as if it weighed several tons, yet still she walked as though some inner directive guided her back to the caravan park and the man with the strange green eyes.

Meriel Harbrow had wakened earlier than usual that morning. She hadn't slept much after Emma had gone; she might as well get to the laundry and hang her washing before other campers claimed all the available space.

She was carrying her basket of washing through the laundry doorway when Emma walked slowly, wearily, back along the path to Simon's caravan.

Meriel wished she didn't feel so guilty. She assured herself she had nothing to feel guilty about. But something about the girl's drooping shoulders, the slow dragging footsteps, gave the older woman a troublesome sense of wrongdoing.

She greeted Emma with a bright, determined smile, but might well have saved herself the trouble. Like a sleepwalker, Emma stumbled towards Simon's caravan.

Inside the van Simon was already cooking breakfast. He glanced at Emma briefly, reached into the refrigerator for bacon, and dropped two more eggs into the frypan.

Emma blinked at him tiredly, then eased herself on to the seat beside the breakfast table. Her eyes were dark-shadowed, all colour gone from lips and cheeks, leaving a grey-white pallor under the honey tan.

She watched Simon cook breakfast, following his movements with enormous, unwavering eyes.

When he put the plate of food in front of her she said faintly, 'You don't need to hire a cook. You do very well yourself.'

He put a plate of toast beside her.

'Tedious, though, isn't it? That's why the Great Intelligence created Eve. You're here to save the mighty male from the tiresome chores of cooking.' He grinned at her cheerfully. 'Men are destined for other things—even primitive man knew that. Me hunt 'em: you cook 'em.'

Emma leaned her chin on one hand and surveyed him glumly.

'Sexist talk!'

'Thought that might wake you up,' he admitted slyly. 'Now, get busy and eat. Then we'll pack and leave. We'll have a quick morning swim, then head north and inland.'

Emma protested wearily, 'I need to sleep.'

'You can sleep on the beach while I swim.'

She really was exhausted. The meal finished, she picked up her plate to take to the sink, and swayed where she stood. Simon caught her and pressed her down into the seat.

'Hold it!' he commanded. 'Sit there while I wash dishes, just this once. A never-to-be-repeated performance.' And when she protested he added drily, 'I've told you before, you're no good to me staggering about as if I beat you every morning. Your presence is designed to make me inconspicuous, not bring down the wrath of all the Meriel Harbrows of this world.'

With what she felt might be the last breath in her body Emma said huskily, 'I suppose you'll tell me why, some day,' and he said 'Maybe,' but it seemed to Emma he wasn't committing himself. He hadn't made any promises yesterday, he wasn't making any today.

He had, it seemed, taken a dislike to the flowered skirt. He made her change into something new; an affair of startling colour-splashes in violet and blue and rose, with a slim wild-rose top; and some of the colour reflected on to the pallor of her face. He even bullied her into adding colour to her lips, and when she'd brushed her hair into glowing softness he looked at her and whistled appreciatively; and Emma managed a cracked laugh.

Silently he handed her the pearl ring, and she replaced it on her finger.

'Now we'd better get moving. We're going to our own special beach for a last swim before we leave.'

He glanced at her teasingly, as if daring her to protest, and because some of Emma's lost spirits had revived with the change of clothing and the donning of the ring, she folded her lips and said stubbornly, 'Can't you swim somewhere else? I don't want to go there.'

'Of course you don't.' He was collecting beach towels. 'Keep away from it,' he added brutally. 'Let it haunt you for the rest of your days. That's what you want, isn't it? To look back at it and feel sorry for yourself.'

'Don't shout at me!' Emma struggled for dignity, pressing her lips together to stop their shaking.

'I wasn't shouting. I was—er—expressing an opinion.'

'You were shouting!'

He took her chin in his brown fingers, a glimmer of a smile in his green eyes, half laughing at her mutinous expression.

'You know, Emma,' his voice was deep and lazy, 'you could develop into a nagging wife.'

She glared at him defiantly.

'Perhaps you'd like to re-think your proposition, then?'

Fingers tightened on her chin, although his expression remained lazy and half amused.

'When I do, *if* I ever do, I'll let you know,' he said finally. He took his hand away, but her face remained tilted at the angle he'd turned it to. He flicked her with a cool, cool glance.

'Meanwhile, Emma my dear, remember this.' His eyes narrowed and the glint of tolerance disappeared. They were cold, emotionless and without any vestige of the friendship she had thought him about to offer. Still holding her gaze, he stretched out a quick hand and jerked her arm towards him in one swift movement, holding the third finger of her left hand so that the gold ring with its pearl glinted between them.

'This little bauble binds us together. You made a deal with me, Emma. As long as you wear my ring I expect your loyalty, and your co-operation. Right?'

He dropped her hand and stepped out of the caravan into sunshine, where she heard him exchanging terse politeness with the Harbrows. She stood motionless inside the van.

'I'm not bound to anybody,' she tried to assure

herself, but she knew it wasn't true. 'This little bauble binds us together', he had said, but insight told Emma it wasn't the pearl, however beautiful—not so little, either, nor the bauble he had called it, she thought wryly, twisting it in the light.

What bound her to the tall lean man with the sardonic mouth and the hard green eyes and screening black beard was not the ring or the pearl; it was feeling that bound them together. Especially hers. Much as she disliked him, he was preferable to loneliness on the beach.

He stirred her deepest misgivings, yet she had not been able to turn away from him when she had chosen which direction to go after her flight in the darkness. She had returned to him for security. She could no longer protest that she was being carried away against her will, because she had made a decision . . . She had chosen to remain with him.

Emma sat in the Land Rover while Simon dismantled the annexe and prepared the caravan for travelling. And when they finally drove away, the caravan hooked on to the Land Rover, Emma looked back and saw only a patch of pale grass among the melaleuca trees to show where they had camped.

Meriel Harbrow was inspecting her washing in the sun, but for some reason she couldn't understand, Emma didn't want to look at Meriel as they passed. She stared straight ahead all the way to the driftwood beach. It still seemed to Emma's lacerated feelings that Simon had chosen the beach deliberately to upset her, and she found it hard to hold back tears.

'Couldn't you swim somewhere else?'

'No.' He switched off the ignition and opened the door for her.

'I don't see why not.'

Her lips trembled in childish reaction to threat, but he ignored her misery as they scrambled down the cliff-path and on to the sand. Then he tossed her a towel.

'You can sleep. I'll wake you when I come out.' Curiously, Emma watched the tall brown man run into the water. Despite suspicion and dislike, she was drawn to him. He body-surfed the waves; they were coming in swift and strong, and she watched him appearing and disappearing in the churning water.

The boys on their surfboards looked more spectacular, but Simon flung himself into the waves and fought them in hand-to-hand combat. He harnessed the wave he wanted and rode it all the way to shore, staggering out of the pounding white water shaking his head and panting for breath.

Afterwards, when he strode out of the water towards her, Emma saw that he had lost tension. The green eyes glinted.

He said, 'You didn't sleep,' and Emma answered, 'No; but I'm going to,' and as he squatted beside her he shot her a swift look, eyes glinting with humour.

'Are you, now?'

Vigorously he dried his body. He asked suddenly, 'Anybody ever call you Emerald? That's your name, isn't it?'

She shook her head. 'I wouldn't let them.'

'Pity.' He was rubbing sparkling drops from his arms. 'It's a very musical name. Romantic, too. Your mother was right.'

'Hah!'

He was looking out across the ocean, and Emma wished he would keep doing that—looking away from her. She didn't like him too close. He was still breathing hard, and Emma was so aware of his movements that she sat with her attention focussed on the trickling sand between his toes and the runnels of water streaming down his body, and it seemed to her that he must surely feel her scrutiny, though he gave no sign.

He murmured: 'Blue-green the sky and black the wind, And emeraldine the sea . . . I seem to remember that from the days of my youth.'

'Poetry!' Emma scoffed. 'Waste of time.'

He laughed, turning his head so that she was aware of coloured drops of water beading his eyelashes, shining in the sun.

'Didn't they teach you poetry, Emma, in your schoolroom?'

'They tried, but I wouldn't listen.'

'Why not? You're female. Your mind is supposed to be seething with romantic fancies.'

She rearranged herself on the sand, drawing away from him.

'I was too busy. I didn't have time for imaginings.'

That was true enough. After Willie left home her mother had dived into instant depression, then to complete invalidism. She had been overwhelmed, first by the desertion of her husband, then her son. So she had leaned on Emma without realising the demands she made on her growing daughter.

Emma had found herself responsible for everything—cooking, housekeeping; she'd even acted as one-woman cheer-squad in desperate efforts to pull her mother out of depths of depression.

Emma's final year at high school had included a commerical course. She hadn't any experience, and most employers preferred experience, but she had managed enough work at home to hire a typewriter and support herself.

She had watched her mother become a pale, frail ghost. She had been glad to die, Emma thought. Now there was only Willie, who had abandoned her.

Emma flushed when she turned her head from her reverie and found Simon looking at her quietly. You could never be sure how much Simon guessed; those perceptive eyes assessed so shrewdly.

He said, his voice almost gentle, 'All right, have your sleep. I've got enough breath for a couple more waves. See you in a minute.'

This time Emma didn't watch. She rested her head on Simon's towel and closed her eyes, and very soon the surf-sounds lulled her to sleep.

She awoke to find Simon squatting again beside her, but this time the magic was gone. He stared, brooding, out to sea; and when she stirred he glanced at her impersonally and she saw that right now, at this very moment, she didn't matter to him at all. He had withdrawn into his own thoughts, and she doubted whether they were pleasant ones. The good feelings were gone. While she'd been asleep a black mood had come down on him. His faint smile was a token smile only.

He said, 'Well, Emma, it's about to begin.'

'What's beginning?'

'Your job. You're going to be a good little girl and earn your salary from now on, I hope.'

She looked at him crossly.

'How?'

He shot her a sideways glance, thin lips pressed together in ill-concealed irritation.

'Don't be dumb, Emma. You've already been told what you have to do. You will flutter alongside me, looking like my decorative and plausible reason for embracing the good life. My excuse for travelling in the sun, while the rest of the world works. My—er——'

Emma nodded. 'F-Female attachment.'

It didn't make him laugh. It didn't even make him smile. His voice was sharp.

'That's right.'

Despite the warmth of sun on sand, Emma shivered. She stole a fleeting glance through long curling lashes, then turned away quickly.

'So long as you're not planning arson or murder most foul,' she offered, trying to make it sound like a pleasantry and not a nervous question. Because she didn't like what had happened to Simon while he waited beside her on the beach. His thoughts were black, and they showed in his face. An intense darkness had come down on him, and Emma shivered again as she followed him to the Land Rover on the top of the cliffs. Whatever was she letting herself in for?

He wasn't going to tell her any more. He sat grim and silent while she arranged herself beside him, apparently not noticing that she huddled as far away from him as possible. While he manoeuvred vehicle and van between the trees overhanging the access road, Emma looked over her shoulder and saw the small white beach below. It wouldn't haunt her now; whatever ghosts it had held for her had been exorcised. Her fears were in the Land Rover beside her; the saturnine, bearded man sitting at the wheel as if he listened to his own thoughts and had no time to waste on her trepidations.

Sunlight threw leaf shadows on to the windows. They danced on Simon's cheeks and flecked the curling black beard with fractured sunlight, but his expression remained fixed and remote. He could have been made of granite, Emma thought, he sat so rigidly beside her. Only his hands moved on the steering-wheel.

They drove out of bushland towards the highway, where they swung north; and Emma did not look back because she was afraid that if she did, she might cry, for what she was leaving.

It hadn't been wonderful, but she had a suspicion that it might be a lot easier than whatever she was heading for.

CHAPTER FOUR

EMMA drowsed through most of the long day's drive. The swim had invigorated Simon, so that he seemed to need few breaks on the way, apart from lunch at a small country hotel. After they left the coast, the road twisted over a chain of mountains. Once they passed a massive fern gully, and Emma blinked and said, 'I'd like to explore that some day.' Simon murmured, 'Perhaps you will,' but it didn't sound like a promise; and Emma closed her eyes and settled back fretfully into her corner.

It was late afternoon when they reached a look-out on the peak of a high mountain, and Simon pulled the four-wheel-drive and its attendant caravan into a run-off so that he and Emma could look down on what lay below.

Emma rubbed weariness from her eyes and blinked herself awake. Beside the mountaintop, other peaks threw purple shapes against the sky; but it was the valley below that enchanted her. A long wide valley with a rise and fall of gentle hills. Immediately below the mountain a small town nestled between a road and a river, and the late afternoon sun blazed on masses of flowering gumtrees, scarlet and orange and apricot and white, like colour-splashes on an artist's palette.

Emma leaned forward to peer through the windscreen.

'It's incredibly beautiful!'

Simon gave her a wintry smile.

'Not always.'

Emma shrank back into her corner. Since he was determined to take the lustre from the day, she hadn't strength or desire to cajole him. Let him brood!

After they had traversed the winding mountain road and reached the township Simon pulled in at a small service station for petrol.

The garage proprietor was a large friendly man with amiable, slightly-curious eyes.

'Travelled far?'

Simon answered tersely, 'Not far.'

'Come for the Festival, have you?'

Simon climbed back into the Land Rover without answering and Emma asked determinedly, 'What festival have we come for?'

At first she thought he wasn't going to answer, then he said gruffly, 'Carnival time at Luradil. That's what we're going to see, Emma.'

Anything less like carnival than Simon's grim face Emma couldn't imagine. Yet even as she huddled back into her corner he turned to her again, and this time his voice was more friendly.

'It's one of those little festivals they have in country towns once a year. At least, they held it annually when I lived in the district about five or six years ago.'

That was the first information he had given her . . . that once he had lived here. She pondered over it for a while, thinking questions like 'Why did you leave?' And why have you come back?' but she didn't ask any of them. Simon wasn't really communicating. The reticence he drew about himself was formidable, and she wasn't going to waste her energy trying to penetrate it.

When they arrived at the caravan park and found the sign 'No Vacancies', Emma stared deliberately ahead and let Simon deal with it. It was his problem, not hers.

He leaned across and opened the door for her.

'Go and look around the town. Wander up and down the main street and see if you can buy some take-away food. I'll meet you in front of the post office in an hour. You can manage to find the post office, I take it?'

She glared at him defiantly.

'If I can't, I'll shed my clothes and dance naked down the main street, so you won't have any difficulty finding me. Just look for the crowd.'

Afterwards, she was sorry she had said that. It was a juvenile thing to say, but Simon made her feel like that sometimes.

The street was thronged with people, although the carnival had not yet started. There were carpenters hammering stalls and booths, men on ladders stringing up decorations and coloured lights. Despite weariness, Emma found herself excited.

She found a hamburger shop and collected their evening meal in brown paper bags that stayed warm in her hands; then she located the post office and waited for Simon, under the lacy green leaves of two jacaranda trees.

He said mildly, 'If that's my supper, I hope you

don't plan to sit on it,' and she flushed and handed him the bags.

He raised quizzical eyebrows. 'Hamburgers! No chicken?'

Something had happened to please him. He was actually smiling.

Emma said cautiously, 'There's probably a chicken place somewhere, but I didn't find it. I thought we could sit under the trees and eat them. I found a beautiful park, Simon.'

He nodded thoughtfully.

'I know—down by the river. But we'll have to see it tomorrow. There's a shortage of camping space and I had to finish up parking the van in somebody's back yard. I promised to take you back and introduce you.'

He led her down a side street to a square timbered house set well back from the road. The house was surrounded by a wide verandah trellised in morning glory vines with blue-purple trumpets; and along the driveway two lines of peppertrees trailed slender branches. Simon had parked his van under the trees with a long power-cord connecting it to the house; and after they had eaten the hamburgers, Emma combed her hair and freshened her face.

Memories of Meriel Harbrow made her nervous about meeting new people, but as she and Simon walked towards the verandah the back door of the house opened, and Emma found she needn't have been apprehensive.

A slender girl in a green cotton dress carried a teapot of tea to a table on the verandah, and behind her an equally slight young man bore a tray with wine and glasses. The girl smiled as she came through the doorway and her clear silver voice called a welcome.

'Glad you could join us. Will you have tea, coffee or wine? Or all three?'

Simon said, 'Valerie and Len Farrow—my fiancée, Emma,' and Emma felt a small shock of surprise at the expression.

Valerie Farrow had a wide uptilted mouth, clear blue eyes and a sprinkling of freckles on lightly-tanned cheeks. She had short blonde hair, cleverly cut, and after they had settled themselves on the verandah she explained to Emma that she worked as a hostess during the festival at the Delrayo Winery, on the other side of the valley.

Val had the warmth and ready smile and confidence of one who likes people; she was frankly interested in Simon and Emma, where they had come from, where they were going.

Emma evaded most of the friendly questions as well as she could, and whenever she floundered Simon leaned forward from where he sat with Len, farther along the verandah, and smoothly filled in. They'd come from the coast, he explained, to see the festival. As to where they were going, they hadn't decided. Probably back to the coast, to get married.

Emma felt guilty about the subterfuge, but Valerie readily accepted Simon's explanations.

Her husband, Len, was redhaired with a sharp, clever face. He was employed, he explained, as advertising and publicity officer at the Winery.

'You must visit the Winery on one of the open

days,' he enthused. 'Val can escort you on one of the tours, and explain what wine-making is all about.'

Emma cried, 'That would be lovely. I didn't know you could do that.' And Simon drawled, 'Yes; we've planned a visit on Sunday afternoon'.

And because they had both spoken together, contradicting each other, Emma felt embarrassed. Simon should have told her they were going to the vineyards, then she wouldn't have made that silly remark. It made her feel childish and awkward, although Valerie and Len appeared not to notice.

Emma quietened then, sitting back and listening to talk about wineries and vineyards. To her surprise, Simon seemed to know a great deal about them. She had an uneasy suspicion that he was guiding the conversation, using these two pleasant people to secure information, although he did it innocently enough.

Now, more than ever, sitting on the verandah in the fading light, Emma felt Simon's remoteness. She knew his detachment was deliberate, that he withheld himself, except for a surface friendliness that must have attracted Len, for he was talking freely to Simon about the Winery and its management.

Simon was saying blandly, 'Slipping a bit, aren't they, at Delrayo's? I've heard rumours that profits are down and they aren't doing so well the last couple of years.'

'Not a bit of it.' Len filled glasses, pouring for Emma and Valerie too, as they finished their pot of tea. 'Our Winery's doing better than ever. I've only been here four years, but every year has been a good harvest. Delrayo wines are winning more awards than ever at the shows. Our winemaker is a man from California, and he's producing some really outstanding blends. Crops good, markets expanding, what more could you ask?'

'Nothing.' Simon's voice was almost a whisper.

'I don't know the figures, of course. I'm not on that side of it. The Board consists of members of the Delrayo family. Douglas Delrayo is manager and secretary.'

Twilight was making Simon's face a blur in darkness to Emma, but she heard the careful control in his voice as he remarked that he was pleased to hear it . . . and a little surprised.

'It's not what I heard,' he said again. 'I was told they've over-extended in purchasing equipment—stuff like mechanical harvesters and stainless steel fermentation tanks. And that they'll be in a spot of bother for a while until they recoup expenses.'

Len laughed.

'No way,' he contradicted. 'You've heard wrongly, that's for sure. Come and see for yourself on Sunday. You can taste, too, You'll be impressed, I'm sure, if you know anything about wines?'

The last was a query and Simon nodded. 'A little,' he confessed; but Emma had a strong suspicion it was more than a little. She wasn't at all surprised when Simon added, 'I've been overseas the last few years, working in vineyards in Italy and France and Spain. And I spent a while in California. I have investments in grape-growing—

a friend of mine is interested——'

'Was it your friend who told you Delrayo's were going bad?'

'No.' Simon tasted the wine Len had poured for him, and nodded appreciatively. Len pushed the bottle towards him.

'I'll introduce you to the wine-maker—the bloke from California.'

'Not one of the Delrayo family?'

'No. Young Carne Delrayo is his assistant. Carne will take over the laboratory eventually, though he has a bit to learn yet. The American bloke, Ed Stainsh, plans to move on after a few years.'

It was talk from a strange world to Emma. Ordinarily, she would have found it fascinating, but Simon's devious probing was making her uncomfortable.

Unlike Meriel Harbrow, Valerie showed no sign of considering anything odd about the relationship between the tall, taciturn man and the so-much-younger girl.

She touched the pearl on Emma's finger lightly.

'That's lovely, isn't it? Did you choose it, or did Simon?'

'I chose it.'

Emma hoped Valerie wouldn't notice her confusion, but the other girl was intent on examining the ring.

'So clever of you not to choose something ordinary. But I think you'd always select the unusual, wouldn't you?'

Emma heard the surprise in her own voice.

'I don't know. I never thought about it.'

'Oh yes,' Val nodded confidently. 'I'm dealing with people all the time at the Winery. I can tell. You have flair.'

Emma was relieved to talk to Valerie about their trip from the coast and the beaches they had seen, until Simon stood up, signifying it was time for them to say goodnight.

He and Emma used the bathrooms in the house; and later as she pattered quickly down the drive-way under the peppertrees and into bed, Emma had a pleasant feeling of ease, as if she might have reached at last a place where she might, some day, belong.

Lying in bed, watching the peppertrees swaying outside the caravan window, she drifted to sleep.

She must have been sleeping deeply, because the sounds that eventually awakened her seemed to come from another planet. They dragged her awake so gradually that when she finally sat up, blinking and rubbing her eyes, she wasn't entirely sure whether they had been real or whether she had imagined them. She listened intently.

At first, nothing disturbed the silence. Then in the annexe where Simon slept Emma heard low, murmuring sounds of distress; a restless gasping, as though something or someone struggled for breath. Then a series of small whispering groans, a low whimpering like a child crying in the night for attention. Then another silence.

Emma climbed out of bed and quietly opened the caravan door. Moonlight seeped in through Simon's small window and on to his peaceful face.

She didn't want to shine the torch and disturb him, but there was not enough moonlight to show the corners.

Whatever had called out must still be there. There had been no scuffling to suggest retreat. Then, just as she reached for the torch, Emma saw the peace vanish from Simon's features. His head jerked restlessly against the folded sleeping-bag he used as a pillow. His strong brown hands clenched on the blanket he had thrown over his hips while his mouth made small gasping sounds of protest. Simon was dreaming, and his dreams were not pleasant.

Emma leaned over him, watching him turn and twist. Impulsively she reached out and touched one of his flailing hands, and when his fingers closed around hers she knelt beside him, trying not to feel the pain of his grip on her fingers. The mutterings ceased.

Emma was disengaging herself to creep back into the caravan when suddenly Simon reached out for her. Eyes still closed in sleep, he pulled her towards him, breathing fast as he forced her down until she lay alongside him. She felt the coarse springy hair of his beard brushing her cheek.

Horrified, Emma caught her lower lip between her teeth. She dared not pull away from him. Her feelings were a mixture of fear for herself, and pity for the man who clutched her.

This was not the way her mother had needed her. Her mother had cried for the reassurance of Emma's presence in the house; in the rattle of dishes, the tapping typewriter, the sound of footsteps.

But Simon needed to touch. He pressed his body against hers, forcing her closer so that she was aware of the hard-muscled diaphragm, the body movements as he turned. She wore only the flower-patterned shirt Simon had given her, and through it she felt the play of muscle and tendons as his arm curved over her. With the other, he caressed her, demandingly at first, then slowly and tranquilly as if he absorbed peace and pleasure from her soft, smooth skin. As he relaxed, Emma tensed.

She was caught in his arms now, head close to his chin, so that again she felt the dark hair curling against her mouth. One of his hands came to rest heavily, palm down, on the bare flesh between her hips. She was shatteringly aware of it.

Emma waited tensely for him to go back to sleep. His breathing slowed, and carefully she lifted the arm and laid it over his own body. She had almost wriggled herself free when he lurched forward in a sudden, violent movement and his mouth came down on her mouth, crushing-cruel at first, as though some demon drove him against her; then the contact grew gentler.

She had never fancied that dark beard, yet now it brought a multitude of pleasant sensations as it brushed her skin. His lips teased hers, while one hand traced the rises and hollows of throat and breast, touching . . . touching . . . He moved, and she felt the murmur of his lips against her face. 'Caro . . . Caro . . .'

It wasn't her name that he whispered, but Emma

lay suddenly bathed in a wave of pleasure. Every cell of her body tingled with sensation.

She opened her eyes to find him blinking down at her, watching the recognition as his forehead creased in almost comical surprise.

'Emma!'

Fiercely he thrust her away from him. The hands that had caressed her became hard and impersonal as he swung to sitting position and sent her tumbling on to the matting floor.

'Go back to bed!'

Emma's face was calm, but she had to moisten swollen lips with her tongue before she could answer him.

'All right.'

Not without dignity, she gathered the crumpled shirt around her and walked towards the caravan door.

'Emma?'

She turned back and found him sitting, knees bent, watching her. To her surprise his voice was gentle.

'Emma. Were you lonely?'

She had reached the doorway now, standing with one foot on the metal step, a hand on the door-latch. She looked back over her right shoulder, shaking her head. He watched intently.

'Sure?'

'I'm okay. Don't worry.'

She whispered it softly, before she went inside and closed the door.

In a wall-mirror near the bed, Emma looked at her reflection with wonder: at her lips, soft and swollen because Simon Charles had kissed them; at her long slim throat that his suntanned fingers had fondled; at her body which he had teased, and which now felt unfamiliar because Simon Charles had touched it.

She carried the sensations of pleasure to bed with her. One thing she could be certain of: the tall suntanned man with the green eyes was no beginner in the art of lovemaking. Even in sleep his hands had moved over her body with skill and assurance.

Outside in the annexe, Simon slept peacefully. He made no more cries of pain or anguish in the night. Emma knew, because she did not sleep again. All her senses had been sharpened so that she became acutely aware of every sound, every movement, in or around the caravan. If a blade of grass had bent and straightened in the light breeze, she believed she would have heard it. She had never been so alive before. Even the brushing of Simon's shirt against her skin set it tingling. She lay awake until morning; and when the first light filtered through the peppertrees outside her window, she rose and dressed; and had breakfast waiting for Simon when he woke.

When he came into the caravan Simon stood looking at her. He said, 'Smells good' but made no move to sit down. Emma felt he might have been embarrassed, and perversely decided to let him make the first move.

He said finally, 'Tell me, Emma—I don't suppose you'd care to discuss with me what brought on that little episode last night?'

Emma put his breakfast on the table.

'You were having a nightmare,' she said briefly.

That startled him. He sat down and buttered his toast; and after a while he said, 'You'd better stand guard over those maternal instincts of yours.' When Emma looked at him blankly he added sternly, 'They could get you into a lot of trouble.'

Emma poured cereal into a bowl, added milk, and sat down opposite him at the table. When she said nothing he continued grimly, 'Next time, just let me yell, or whatever it was I was doing. I don't need a rescuer.' He gave a faint grin, then, and added enigmatically, 'You were lucky to get away unscathed.'

Emma thought that closed the subject, but when breakfast was eaten he carried his dishes to the sink.

'Where's the tea? I'll pour it for you.' As he put the cup and saucer beside her, he said with a quick, half-humorous quirk of the lips, 'I hope my amorous advances didn't upset you, Emma.'

She sugared her tea and stirred it calmly.

'Don't apologise. You've already told me I'm not your type.'

He murmured softly, 'I could have been mistaken. Sometimes a man can be a little hasty.'

She stared at him across the table to see whether he was joking, but he stirred his tea, watching the ripples in the teacup. After a few moments he added gently, 'A man would have to be low, wouldn't he, seducing a maiden under those conditions?' and when she made no reply he added even more softly, 'You *are* a maiden, Emma, I take it?'

Emma put down her teacup with a clatter.

'If you mean am I a v-virgin—yes, I am.' She stared at him defiantly, cheeks flushing.

'I thought all you kids who live in communes sooner or later got around to——'

Her voice was crisp.

'Not all of us. Anyway, it wasn't a commune. It was a house.'

A derelict house, she ought to have said, but she wouldn't. He didn't have to know they were squatters, in addition to everything else. 'And sometimes it was the beach', she could have added; but she didn't say that either.

When she looked up at him again he had both eyebrows raised. She saw the quick movement.

'Don't tell me nobody ever asked you?'

Emma glowered at him.

'Somebody did ask me. And for your information, I said No.'

So now he knew she was inexperienced at lovemaking. Though this was the first time she'd ever felt embarrassed about it, or thought very much about it at all. Now he'd decide she was a greenhorn. Well, she was; and he might as well know it.

He wouldn't want her now, and that was a very good thing, because she certainly didn't want him.

Next time he called out in the night—if there ever was a next time, which she doubted—he would push her away quickly before those lean hands stirred her body into clamouring sensations she neither liked nor understood; before he coaxed her into torrents of feeling that threw her off balance and out of control . . . She didn't want that sort of thing happening to her.

When she found the courage to look at him again, he was watching her across the table, as if he knew what she had been thinking. The emerald green eyes were rich and deep, the sensuous mouth half soft with laughter. But he said nothing as Emma stood hastily and began clearing the table. As she pumped water into the sink, he picked up the teapot to empty it outside. The glitter was back in his eyes again.

'Emma—about last night. I hope you didn't find the experience too disagreeable?'

His brows lifted in mocking question. Emma steeled herself. Desperately, she contrived a careless shrug. Her limpid eyes met his innocently.

'Oh—so-so!' She managed another careless shrug, and choked back a laugh at his stunned expression. But he recovered swiftly.

'So-so, was it, you young brat!' He made a mock-lunge at her; but when she added thoughtlessly, 'Even if you did think I was somebody else,' he gave her a sudden icy stare. This was not the time, nor the place, to ask who was Caro.

He disappeared, and with a small smile tugging her lips Emma went back to her dishwashing.

That ought to have shown him she wasn't going to put up with any nonsense. He could keep his teasing to himself from now on.

Nevertheless, she gave a quick anxious glance at the shelf where she had placed the pearl ring while she worked. It was too valuable to lose, she excused herself. She had to keep an eye on it. Not because it had special meaning for her, but if she lost it Simon would be angry, and from what she'd seen of him if he ever became really angry she, Emma, wouldn't want to be there.

Yet when he came back with the empty teapot he smiled at her, easily if briefly.

'Hurry up. Time to go into town. The festival opens officially tonight. Let's get our shopping done before more hordes of people come pouring in.'

He didn't ask if she wanted to go. It was probably part of her job. Emma sighed, and followed him dutifully.

Already the main street was thronged with people. Booths and stalls were being stocked; a pop group played disco music under the flowering gums, and street decorations fluttered in a light, warm summer breeze.

Shopping finished, Simon and Emma wandered around inspecting the stalls. Emma sensed a new alertness in Simon. He walked lazily beside her, admiring hand-crafted jewellery and paintings, potted plants and handprinted materials—yet all the time he missed nothing.

From behind the disguising sunglasses Emma saw that he studied every face and listened to every voice. It wasn't that he withdrew his entire attention from her. He even bought pearl earrings from a jewellery stall under the jacaranda trees. But all the time he scanned the crowds, concentrating so that he overlooked no word, or face, or action that might be of significance to him.

Emma did not want the earrings, but Simon

insisted. When she protested he snapped testily, 'Look, they match the ring. So take them, and be quiet for a change.'

The stallholder, a large apple-cheeked woman in a purple caftan, held them beside Emma's ring and nodded.

'Perfect,' she wheedled. 'You have excellent taste, sir.'

Emma looked swiftly at Simon through the curl of her lowered lashes, expecting the blatant flattery to put him off. But he clinched the deal, and pushed the earrings into her hand. Emma took them reluctantly.

'When and where will I ever wear pearl earrings?' she demanded, and Simon replied casually, 'Tonight, for starters.'

Emma stood stock still, planting herself in front of him.

'Don't tell me anything.' She shook her head, and he reached out and tilted her chin, patting it as though they had been friends for years, Emma thought. She glared her exasperation, and he leaned down and planted a swift kiss on her forehead.

'Emma, I'm sorry. I do forget things sometimes. Anyway, I was half minded to keep it as a surprise, but since you insist on knowing everything, here it is. We're dining out tonight, at one of the local hotels, the large one in the centre of town. I booked a table for the festival dinner.'

Her eyes widened. 'Whatever for?'

'Emma, don't argue. You're dining out with me, because I want to be there. That's enough, isn't it?'

His voice softened. 'You can give your new evening dress its first public appearance. *And* your earrings. Agreed?'

Her new dress! In the confusion of their departure from Jerinda, Emma had left the unopened box in the bottom of the caravan wardrobe. That afternoon she opened it, and shook out the dress; a slim creation of five slender frills of white chiffon, falling in delicate tiers, one above the other. The top frill formed a bodice with tiny sleeves and a scoop neckline where one white chiffon rose nestled on one side. A young girl's dress—a dream dress. Emma touched it reverently.

She borrowed Val's iron to press the white chiffon. The material was so fragile she hardly dared touch it, the falling tiers featherlight as she smoothed them.

Simon travelled well, for all his casual appearance. Emma saw that he had tailored slacks and jackets, silk Italian shirts among the casual gear, and several rollneck jumpers.

Because it seemed important to Simon, Emma took care over her dressing. Valerie let her prepare inside the house. Emma brushed her hair until it shone, and fixed the pearl earrings in place.

Valerie, laughing and confident in a swirling dress of apple-green taffeta, with an opal necklace, had already blow-waved her own hair. Emma said wistfully, 'I wish I looked like you.' The other girl laughed.

'Take a look in the mirror. You won't want to make any changes!'

Gravely Emma studied her reflection. The layered dress was candle-slim, falling in the five soft tiers from shoulders to ankles. From the cloud of brown-gold hair her pale oval face with its glowing eyes and soft sweet mouth showed uncertainty. Certainly she looked different from the girl Simon had rescued on the beach. But would he like it?

As though sensing Emma's doubts, Valerie said softly, 'You look angelic.'

Emma laughed.

'I don't want to look *that* different!'

'But you don't really want to look like everybody else, do you?'

Emma stared at her reflection hesitantly.

'I don't know,' she admitted. 'Are you sure I don't look overdressed?' She touched the layers of chiffon diffidently. 'I feel unreal.'

'So? Aren't you lucky?'

Simon in his tailored slacks and dark reefer jacket, with the white silk rollnecked jumper, was grander than Emma expected, and she glanced at him apprehensively. But he supported her elbow in a show of gallantry as they entered the hotel, and in the contact she found reassurance. Emma need not have been concerned about her appearance. There were many women in the dining-room of the hotel with gowns more elaborate than hers. This was a gala occasion.

Crystal chandeliers glittered, and tables gleamed with crystal and white lace and polished silverware. Valerie and Len sat at the main table in the centre of the large dining-hall, where the Delrayo family—owners of the local winery, as Len had explained, and 'nearly everything else around here'—were guests of honour.

Len, because of his employment at the winery, was included in the list of official guests, but, as he admitted with a friendly chuckle, he and Val would be earning their keep, as he expressed it—entertaining interstate and overseas guests and buyers.

The small table that Simon had booked was hidden in the shadows of an obscure corner, well outside the bright glitter from the chandeliers. Apart from a small golden wall-light, their table remained dim, while they had a perfect view of the dining area. Emma suspected Simon had wanted it so.

The waiter offered wine 'from our local winery' and Simon, a strange smile flickering, supervised the pouring. He said teasingly, 'Perhaps you'd prefer lemon squash, Emma?' but she shook her head. She might be ignorant and inexperienced, but she could appreciate the touch and taste of pleasure as well as he could.

She challenged him after the waiter had gone: 'You don't know what I like. You don't know anything about me.'

And the gloom must have lifted for him, because he smiled broadly, white teeth flashing in the mysterious darkness of the bearded face.

'I must take the trouble to find out some day.' He handed her the menu. 'Meanwhile, you'd better decide what you want to eat, since I'm not knowledgeable enough to choose for you.'

'You can order,' she replied briefly. She didn't want him criticising her choice of food. He selected seafood cocktail, with bream for entrée, followed by orange duck, and she nodded approval.

Simon seemed especially interested in the guests at the main table. He leaned back idly, apparently relaxed, but Emma knew he had not been really relaxed at any time since their arrival at Luradil. Always, he was looking and listening; and tonight was no exception.

Emma let her attention wander after Simon's to the guests of honour; women in expensive gowns and sparkling jewellery; men well tailored, with an air of prosperity and confidence, even a faint tinge of superiority that made Emma's skin prickle.

'Snobs,' she decided acidly, faintly resentful.

She entertained herself while she ate, trying to guess which of the beautiful people interested Simon, but she couldn't tell. That keen, speculative gaze lingered first on one, then the other, as though he could not see enough of them.

Emma wasn't used to glittering occasions, and she studied this one curiously. She knew already from Len and Valerie that the head of the Delrayo family would not be present. Philip Delrayo was an invalid, confined to a wheelchair, and his wife Irene stayed almost always by his side.

A cool and beautiful blonde attracted Emma's attention; superbly gowned in a revealing creation of peacock blue, she wore a diamond necklace that outshone the chandeliers. Farther along the table Emma noticed a girl about her own age, strikingly dressed in what must surely have been a model gown. Bare neck and shoulders gleamed above cunningly-cut scarlet jersey, sleek black hair pulled skilfully into a shining roll that allowed the diamonds in her ears to glitter freely as she talked. She moved restively, making quick dramatic gestures, and the young man sitting beside her hung on every word and movement as though there was nobody else at the table.

On her other side sat a young man of a very different type. Watching him across the room, Emma caught her breath. He was the most strikingly handsome man she had ever seen. Hair black like Simon's, but straight and smooth, brushed back from a high smooth forehead, features even and beautifully shaped, as though nature had given him the best she had to offer. Eyes strong and arresting, even in the distance, although she could not see their colour. Mouth soft and sensual, upcurving like a girl's. An enchanted young man, Emma decided. Obviously he had everything—looks, background, wealth and confidence. He sat, idly bored, watching the other young man's efforts to please the girl in red . . . watching the girl lead him on. Their antics obviously amused him, though occasionally his attitude lapsed into complete boredom.

Unlike him, the older man at the head of the table concentrated almost desperately on looking after his guests. He had a tense, anxious face, restless eyes and restless hands. Emma felt sorry for him, seemingly so overwhelmed by his responsibility, driven by anxiety not to let his attention lapse lest the whole evening should collapse around him.

Emma thrummed her fingertips on the tablecloth, in time to the music.

'I'd like to dance, Simon. Can we?'

His voice was abstracted.

'I don't dance.'

Emma pouted. He hadn't bothered to say 'Sorry.' Just the terse 'I don't dance', as if her request was of no consequence. He spoke very little throughout the meal, just ate and watched.

'See anyone you know?' she asked once, daring to be flippant, but he didn't answer.

So you don't want to talk to me, she thought. That's okay by me. I'll sit here and enjoy myself. I'm not going to beg for your attention . . .

After a dessert of delicious cassata, they drank coffee and sipped more wine. Shadows continued to make mystery of Simon's features, but he had mellowed, and several times he glanced at her and smiled slightly, white teeth flashing, the brooding expression lifting.

Yet he still didn't bother much about talking to her. All he cared about was those people at the main table.

Although later, when they were settling back into the caravan, he said, 'Emma, if you ever do feel compelled to come and rescue me from my nightmares, don't wear that dress. If you do, I shan't be responsible for my actions.'

Emma smiled at him sweetly.

'You like it, then? You actually noticed!' He hadn't paid her much attention all night, and she felt piqued. She twirled provocatively, stirring the layers of slender chiffon and setting them fluttering . . .

He was taking off the reefer jacket, hanging it on a hanger, pushing past her and outside to the annexe.

'Emma, you occasionally show signs of developing into a reasonably intelligent young woman. Don't start being feminine, for God's sake. Practise your wiles somewhere else.'

He pushed her, not very gently, back into the caravan. Emma heard the door click. Peeling off the white dress, she pulled a petulant face. Intelligent sometimes, was she? Not fascinating, like the sleek blonde at the hotel, with her golden hair and sparkling jewels; nor like the striking girl in the startling red dress . . . the girl with the doting young man.

Getting ready for bed, Emma wondered what it would be like to have that kind of power over a man. It would never happen to her. Men didn't lie down and die to please skinny little beach girls who might prefer lemon squash to wine.

But even skinny little beach girls grow up, Emma thought wistfully, hanging the white dress in the wardrobe. She took off the pearl earrings and the ring, putting them away lovingly.

The fates had sent her pearls and a white dress and a man who didn't always notice she was there . . . would they grant her any more favours, with a little luck? Would she grow up beautiful?

There was no sound outside in the annexe. All Simon's demons must have been exorcised last night; all his nightmares gone.

Emma wasn't sure how she would react if it happened again. One thing was certain, she'd know better than to get close enough for those long arms to reach out and grab her and pull her close.

Why then was she smiling softly as she went to sleep?

CHAPTER FIVE

VALERIE was making toast in the kitchen next morning when Emma went into the house. She gave Emma a warm smile.

'Enjoy yourselves last night?'

Emma paused in the doorway. Len, mouth full of toast, waved a cheery hand. Emma answered, 'Every minute—all that delicious food and music, everything looking so marvellous.'

Len managed to mumble through the toast.

'*And* the wine?'

'Yes, that too. Simon told me it came from your Winery.'

'They all do, all the wines for the festival dinner. You can have anything you fancy, within reason, any other time, but of course we hope you'll prefer the local wines. You're coming to the vineyard today?'

'Wouldn't miss it for anything.'

Valerie poured Len a cup of tea, and raised her eyebrows at Emma.

'We didn't see you on the dance floor last night. Don't you like dancing? I was looking for you——'

And Emma said without thinking, 'Yes, I do; I love dancing. I tried to coax Simon to get up, but he kept saying he doesn't dance——'

It was only when the words were out and she saw the quick surprise on Val's face that Emma realised what she had done.

If Simon didn't dance, and they knew each other well enough to be engaged to marry, wouldn't Emma have known long before last night? Valerie covered her surprise swiftly, giving Emma another warm smile.

'Next time, ask Len to save you a couple of dances. He's a very agile fellow, with rhythm in his feet, even if I do say so myself. Aren't you, my love?'

'Thank you. I'll remind you of that little compliment next time I tread on your toes!'

Emma fled to the shower. That had been stupid . . . really dumb. Making that silly remark! She shook herself angrily.

Valerie had been quick to hide her astonishment, but not quick enough.

Emma didn't like acting in front of Len and Val; it seemed deceitful. And the subterfuge had found her out, with her tongue making that silly mistake.

'I must be the first girl,' she thought wryly, 'to become engaged not knowing whether or not her fiancé cared to dance.'

She would have to be careful. That impulsive mistake made her understand there could be no reaching out to other people. She couldn't afford errors that might arouse suspicion; she owed that much to Simon.

Emma sighed as she walked back to the caravan. She liked Val, and Len with his kind, clever face; but there must be no more relaxing.

Glancing at Simon's expression, Emma knew she wasn't going to tell him what she had done. He'd begun cooking breakfast and when she took the pan from him he smiled down at her, a slow lazy smile that stretched his mouth and crinkled his eyes and softened his face. No, she wouldn't disturb that amiability.

She hung her towel on the rail and took over the cooking.

'I suppose I'd better trim my beard.' Simon fondled the wild mass of hair reflectively. 'Might as well look reasonably handsome for you to tote around, I suppose. What do you think, Emma?'

'Why don't you shave it off? It must be hot.'

He closed up then, looking at her with cold eyes.

'Because I need it. I told you, I don't want to be recognised before I've done what I want to do.'

Emma studied him doubtfully.

'You have very distinctive eyes.'

His mouth twitched. 'Been inspecting them, have you?'

'No, I haven't. But you don't see that colour green very often.'

'Just as well it's summer. I can wear sunglasses, with nice dark lenses. That ought to do the trick.'

Emma watched him thoughtfully, sighed, and went back to her cooking.

You could paint yourself purple all over, she was thinking, and whatever's different about you, it would still show through. I would recognise you anywhere . . .

As if he understood what she was thinking he said, 'I've been abroad for the last five years. A man should have changed a bit in that time.'

Emma nodded. Perhaps he had, but she wasn't really convinced.

The beard trimmed looked a little neater, but that was all. Emma said pertly, 'That ought to make the grapes swoon!'

'But not you!'

She didn't like it when he came and stood so close beside her. With Simon, you felt the vibrations when he became approachable. Emma knew about sexy men: that there is a man/woman force that flows between the sexes, and that some men have more of it than others.

She knew that Simon Charles was one of those. The lean, hard body with its tanned skin, the flashing green eyes that changed to slumbrous challenge when he forgot the devil on his shoulder, the sensuous curled mouth, the powerful chest with curling dark hair. And the latent energy that was detectable even when he stood lazily leaning against a doorway, or strolling along a street looking at faces. They combined into a disturbing presence. This was a powerful man, and Emma didn't care for too much power in other people. She found it disquieting.

She did her best to sound unmoved. 'Not you?' he'd queried, and she answered him saucily.

'You'd have trouble making me swoon.'

He leaned over her.

'Would I now? Would I, Emma?'

She stood her ground. He pointed over her shoulder, eyes alight with mockery.

'You're burning the breakfast.'

As she sprang to the rescue she heard the door shut and the sound of his retreating laughter.

*

But on the way to the Winery Simon forgot to tease her. He stopped in Luradil and made her buy another hat, something more protective than the light straw, because one day soon they might go farther inland, where the sun was hot and fierce.

Emma brought a cream stetson, which went oddly with the colour-splashed wrap-around skirt and blue suntop she was wearing. But the wide-brimmed hat sat on her brown hair with a rakish air, and she noticed several people turn to look at her.

Simon went off to shop for himself, and Emma wandered around the street stalls. Under a spreading gumtree smothered in fierce crimson flowers, she found a hand-crafts booth with racks of gold chains and medallions. They were beautifully crafted; each one an Australian bird or animal enclosed in a ring of gold.

Emma chose a golden tern, with long pointed wings and slender streamlined body rocket-shaped for long swift flight and fast diving. Often she had watched the terns along the beaches, plummeting out of the sky to snatch a small fish and dart away again.

She held the chain with its exquisite medallion in the palm of her hand, staring at it in wonder. The jeweller was quick to notice her interest.

He said, 'One of my best efforts, that is. Came out well, didn't it? I nearly kept it myself, but I thought "What the heck! Somebody might like it." '

He wore one golden earring that flashed in the sun, and a scarlet shirt over blue jeans. He gave

Emma a beguiling grin.

'Extra potent charm, that one. Golden protection twenty-four hours a day.'

'Are you sure?'

He flashed her another disarming smile.

'Loaded with luck—they all are. And I had a special feeling about that one, right from the start. I promise you, the luck goes with the bird.'

Emma paid for it out of her wages. When Simon climbed into the Land Rover she said, 'Here's your engagement ring,' and when his forehead creased in an enormous frown Emma realised he imagined she was offering to return the pearl ring. She held out her hand with the gold chain in it and he let out his breath in a light sighing sound and shook his head at her.

But he took the charm, clasping it around his neck under the blue cotton shirt he wore with black jeans. He opened more shirt buttons, and the diving tern glinted bright among the crisp dark hair of his chest.

'Very nice,' he commented, but his expression was non-committal.

Emma said, 'It's lucky,' and he glanced down at it, nodding at the thick mat of hair.

'Lady Luck will need a metal detector to find it!'

Outside Luradil they drove along a yellow gravel side-road, across the river bridge, and over a small rise into the other side of the valley.

The grapevines fluttered green leaves in symmetrical patterns over a gentle rising hillside and flat ground beside the river. Simon pointed out the different varieties among the vines; some with delicate leaves, others heavier, broad-leafed. He was murmuring words like Shiraz . . . Chardonnay . . . Riesling . . .

Emma said helplessly, 'I always thought a grape was a grape, that they were all the same.'

'If you ask Len, he'll tell you the varieties they grow here, and they're always experimenting with new ones. There's a namesake for you, Emma. Emerald Riesling, it's called. I don't know whether they grow it here, but it's grown in other parts of Australia.'

From the car park they walked into the long white Winery, with its notice 'Delrayo Wines' over a white archway. At one end of the building an observation tower climbed into the sky.

As they followed a long line of people into the reception area, Emma felt Simon slipping away from her again. She hoped he wouldn't lapse into moodiness. He had let her get close to him when he teased her at breakfast and she didn't want to be pushed away. Not yet.

He put a hand under her elbow as they waited for a hostess to conduct their tour, and all the way through the processing rooms and down into the cool, dark cellars, he stayed like that: physically close but with his attention roving as though he had forgotten she was there.

Upstairs again the corridor opened into a large wine-tasting room; an opulent room, to Emma's surprise, carpeted and decorated, with stands of bottled wine, and elaborate soft lighting from walls and ceiling. In one alcove there was a display of awards won by the Winery's products. Simon studied each of them intently, while Emma fidgeted. Then he led her to the bar. Emma followed doubtfully.

'Are we going to sample wine?'

'We are.'

Her mouth twisted glumly.

'I wouldn't know where to start,' she confessed.

'Doesn't matter. I think we'll find you a Moselle, that ought to suit your palate.'

The Moselle left warmth and sweetness in Emma's mouth. Valerie, her first tour completed, came to talk.

'What would you like to taste next?'

Emma scanned the wine list doubtfully. 'Shiraz—because I like the name. It sounds like Ali Baba and the Forty Thieves—sort of exotic.'

Faintly smiling, Simon rinsed her glass and poured a little of the Shiraz into it. Emma sipped, pulled a wry face, and found Val and Simon laughing.

'Shiraz is often blended with other varieties. Your deplorable sweet tooth would probably appreciate it better that way.'

He drank the remaining Shiraz, rinsed the glass and poured another white wine for her, this time a sparkling variety.

'I don't like red wines.' Emma felt inept and inexperienced, and the feeling made her cross, but Simon smiled as he handed her the glass.

'You will,' he promised. 'You need educating, young lady.'

So I do, Emma agreed silently. She thought, Your lips and my lips on this one glass, and that's about as close as they'll ever get again, because you're part of all this and I don't know one small thing about it, and why should I care? But she did care, a little. She felt an outsider.

Emma wandered around the room full of people while Valerie talked to Simon about wine-making. Across the room, she discovered the girl with the wilful face from the Festival Dinner. The young man who had danced attendance on her so slavishly wasn't there, but the other one—the extraordinarily good-looking youth with the bored expression—stood talking with her. Both watched the throng of people with the faintly supercilious air of the affluent. The young man was splendid in tailored brown cord slacks and a beige shirt; the girl in figure-hugging lemon with seams slit almost to the thighs, the bodice strapless so that you became instantly aware of perfect figure and beautifully-tanned skin.

She stood alongside a bracket-lamp on the wall with her hair glinting ebony. There was something startling about that jet-black hair. They both had it, the young man and the girl, not curly like Simon's, but sleek and black in an unmistakable bond of kinship.

Emma's glance wandered back to Simon as he stood talking to Valerie at the bar. Len had joined them, too. Simon hadn't taken off the sunglasses. They appeared unnecessary in this cool room with its soft lighting; perhaps he'd forgotten he wore them.

Then Emma saw that she was not the only person watching Simon. The host from the main table at the Festival Dinner—the anxious man—stood not far away from the two raven-haired young people. Half hidden by a display stand, he stared across at Simon as he talked with Len and Valerie; and even in the muted lighting Emma saw clearly the pallid face, the rigid jawline, as he stared across the room at the bearded man lounging against the bar. His hands were clenched into tight fists, and once he swayed as if he might have fallen, but never once did he take that hypnotised stare from the tall man at the bar. As Emma watched, she saw one clenched hand pound the other, as though muscles and sinews tightened in an involuntary movement.

Suddenly apprehensive, she worked her way across the room through the throng of people until she stood behind Simon. She slid a hand into the angle of his bent arm, as he held the wineglass; and he looked down at her and smiled in faint surprise, quite calmly, so that a little of her fear subsided, but only a little.

As Len poured wine into their glasses Emma whispered, 'Simon, that man over there—he's staring at you. I don't like him.'

'Perhaps I remind him of someone. Or maybe he's allergic to beards. Some people are, you know.'

Emma pulled her arm away from him.

'You're absurd!'

'You'll find I'm right. He's probably staring at somebody else.'

Emma frowned. 'Perhaps,' she said, but she didn't believe it, and she wasn't convinced he did, either.

A man's face didn't blanch, not like that, as if every drop of blood had surged back to his frightened heart, just because he was reminded vaguely of somebody. Only if he were certain—if he knew he was threatened.

Emma tried to shake away the feeling of foreboding. She was here to enjoy herself. But all the wine tasted sour, now. She stole a fleeting look at Simon's face, so much of it hidden by the masking beard; the hard green eyes glittering, even behind the sunglasses; the dark high forehead beneath the curling hair; the hawk nose and harsh, bitter mouth that sometimes was not harsh at all, but soft and beautiful

He looked at her over the rim of his wineglass, one eyebrow raised in the familiar gesture. He lowered the glass a little, his lips smiled briefly, but it was not the teasing smile he offered when he became really approachable.

He turned to the bar to speak to Len, and Emma stepped determinedly between him and the man who stared. She felt easier then, as though she might be averting some kind of danger. She knew it was ridiculous, but the thought was there.

Emma did not look across the room to search out the watching man. Once or twice her skin prickled uncomfortably, as if he still stood there, staring. It took all her willpower not to search him out. She was relieved when Valerie led them away to the foot of a narrow spiralling staircase.

'Tradition says the first Delrayo used the tower as an overseer's post, to see what his workers were doing among the vines. We use it now only to let visitors see the fantastic view. You mustn't miss it,' she urged. 'I'd take you myself, but I've another tour starting about now.'

Emma followed Simon reluctantly up the tiny narrow stairs. The surrounding walls were bricks, cunningly cut and interlocked so that they hugged the staircase in a tight spiral. Simon reached for her hand and tugged her up the last few steps.

'You're treading in the steps of several generations of Delrayos, and not one of them was ever murdered in the tower!'

Emma didn't ask him how he knew. She followed docilely across the polished floor made uneven by the treading of countless feet. She looked out, with him, over acres of growing vines, green in the sun, and to the sleepy river with its willows and river gums along green banks.

In the nursery corner, where young rootlings showed fresh and green, irrigation pipes threw huge feathers of spray. Emma said, 'It's beautiful, very pretty,' and shivered, although she could not think why.

Simon's piercing eyes searched every field, assessing area and layout, the flourishing vines in their perfectly-tended symmetry.

Emma waited until he had seen all he wanted, then thankfully followed him down the stairs again and into sunlight.

'Lunch,' he announced. 'Sandwiches and wine. How does that suit you?'

They sat on the riverbank and ate their sandwiches and drank their wine, and slowly Simon came back from wherever or whatever it was that had required most of his attention. He teased Emma about the wine; coaxed her to eat her share of sandwiches.

'What do you think of it, Emma?'

'I'd like to see the grapes harvested. Could we come back when they're ripe?'

'It wouldn't do you much good. They're harvested at night, from midnight until early morning, to cut down oxidation. And there isn't any grape-treading any more. It's all done mechanically here. The harvester works by vibration. It shakes the grapes off the vines—that's more thorough than hand-picking.'

'Is this the kind of place you get your money from?'

'Exactly.' His voice carried a forbidding tone that warned Emma not to ask more questions.

'Can we have a swim in the river?'

'Straight after lunch? Don't be daft. I'm not going to get wet tugging you out of the water again.'

She pulled a face at him, turned on her side, and pillowed her head on one arm. Later when she awoke she found that Simon, too, had relaxed on the grass. He lay on his back, one arm outflung so that it brushed the hem of her coloured skirt, fingers curled as if they might, before he slept, have closed upon the flowered folds. Emma observed him curiously.

The stern face, so formidable when things displeased him, smoothed out in sleep. The features, what you could see of them, were more arresting than handsome, the firm straight nose, dark-fringing eyelashes, crisp dark hair, combined into an intriguing suggestion of sensitivity that wasn't noticeable when he was alert and active, making his scathing remarks, or withdrawing into sombre silences.

He woke then, as if he sensed her staring. As he stretched and rolled over, the gold chain with its diving bird tangled in a tuft of grass.

'I'd better take this thing off before I break it.'

Emma cried sharply, 'Keep it on. You mustn't take it off!' and was surprised by the shrillness of her own voice. She added quickly, 'It's a lucky charm; the man said so. Golden protection twenty-four hours a day.'

That amused him. But he untangled the chain and replaced it around his neck under the blue shirt, the way he might have pleased a child.

Emma couldn't understand her own reaction. Lucky charms . . . protective mascots . . . they'd never been necessary to her before. Why then did she feel this need for security today?

She waited silently as Simon gathered up lunch remnants and fed the swans, then she followed him to the car park.

But all the way back to the caravan, feelings of disquiet rode with her. Silently she prepared the evening meal and when it was over she asked, 'Where are we going tomorrow?' hoping he would say 'Nowhere.'

Instead, he drummed fingers on the table and

fidgeted a little. Then he asked suddenly, 'How would you like to see a rodeo, Emma?'

'Where? Here?'

'Nope.' He shook his head. 'There's a cattle station inland, a homestead called Duelgumbah. We'll need to leave well before dawn in the morning, so it's early night for both of us.'

Emma said carefully, 'Funny name, Duelgumbah. Aboriginal, I guess. What's it mean? Something about gumtrees?'

She didn't want to see a rodeo. She wanted to stay where she was, but she didn't like to mention it.

Simon shook his head.

'No, nothing to do with gumtrees. Duelgumbah is aboriginal for "The Place of the Eel with Wings."'

'Never heard of him. All the eels I've ever met were restricted to fins.'

'Not this one. He's a gigantic creature who lived in the Aboriginal dreamtime, in the local river. He was very special because he had magnificent rainbow-coloured wings that he unfurled whenever he got angry or frustrated. He could cause a drought just by fanning his wings and drying up all water. And he could fly away with all the wild animals that supplied food. So he became a very privileged eel.'

'Tell me,' asked Emma.

'Well, of course, being so powerful and awe-inspiring, he demanded, and got, special privileges from the tribes who lived round about, and from all who walked over his land. They were continually striving to please him, and after a while they grew very sick of his demands. He became so unreasonable that anger overcame their fear. And then one day he made his most outrageous demand. He claimed the most attractive maiden in the tribe, because he was tired of living alone in the river.'

'So what happened then?'

'The tribal elders met to discuss the demand and to select the maiden, who turned out to be the daughter of the local medicine man. He, being unwilling to sacrifice his daughter, persuaded five of the elders to help him clothe the maiden in a kangaroo-skin cloak under which she carried many presents to the winged eel. Hidden among them was a spear, together with a drink made from wild honey laced with something from local berries to make the eel sleep. So then he could be speared to death and the tribes freed from his unreasonable demands.

'Unfortunately the eel, who was very perceptive, refused to go to sleep. He was so intimidating that the maiden dropped the spear, and the eel discovered the plot.

'He turned the five sneaky elders into rocks, and imprisoned the medicine man behind a waterfall, where he babbles to this day. I'll show you the rocks tomorrow, and I may even let you listen to the waterfall. I presume it's still there.'

Emma leaned her chin on cupped hands, watching him silently. The green eyes were veiled, the sensuous mouth softened from its habitual harshness. She searched his expression for laughter and found none.

His hands, lean and brown, with long tanned fingers intertwined, lay on the table. For once she had the feeling that she held his whole attention.

'You made it up!' she said finally.

'Emma!' The thunder in his voice surprised her. 'I do not make things up.'

'What happened to the girl, then? You forgot all about her, didn't you? Or didn't she matter?'

'The girl?' Simon leaned towards Emma, and the softness was gone now from his beautiful mouth.

Emma stared at him defiantly.

'The maiden. The one who set him up,' she reminded him. 'I suppose he drowned her too. Or turned her into stone.'

'He did neither. He was an ingenious eel. He never repeated himself. He grabbed the two-timing maiden with a twitch of his tail, unfurled his shimmering wings, and flew up into the sky until he disappeared from the sight of even the keenest eyes of the tribe. He flew day and night, until he reached a far corner of the sky. He found a great black hole and when it was dark he dumped the maiden beside it and left her there, so close to the edge that if she moved a finger she'd fall in. Then he flew back home and polished his wings in the river.'

'Nasty!' Emma hunched her shoulders and studied Simon thoughtfully. 'I bet you made that bit up, too.'

With one of the quick, lithe movements she had grown to expect from him, Simon left the table and moved towards the caravan door.

'I'll show you,' he promised. 'Some dark night.

Two tiny stars, billions of miles away; those are her eyes. She's still there. And if the night is very, very black you can sometimes see a faint gleam beside her. That's the flash of her spearhead. The eel left it with her. Not that he thought she'd have much use for it up there in the sky. He probably thought it was a good reminder. Or perhaps he left it as a joke.'

Emma tossed her head.

'Not very funny,' she commented.

'No, it wouldn't be much fun, would it? But then she was a poor silly maiden, wasn't she?'

He was jeering at her. Yet suddenly with a fierce movement he stepped towards Emma, leaned down and cupped her face in his two strong hands. His fingers hurt, and he tilted her face roughly towards his, leaning down so that he almost bent double. His lips were so close she felt the light feathering of his breath.

'The high cost of betrayal,' he murmured softly. 'Don't forget that, Emma. There she is, billions of miles away, for ever lonely. Two big stars are her frightened eyes. Doomed to sit for ever, afraid to move. How would you like that?'

She pushed his hands away from her face.

'Trust you to be unpleasant,' she scowled, 'and spoil everything!'

When he had gone she rubbed her fingers along the jawline where his hands had grasped. The skin still tingled.

CHAPTER SIX

THE drive to Duelgumbah next morning brought another unapproachable mood down on Simon. He hustled Emma out of the caravan into darkness and by dawn they were well on their way.

Kangaroos paused from their eating to stare thoughtfully at the passing vehicle. Gentle-eyed, long ears pricked in harmless curiosity, they stood erect. Remembering the motherless joeys at the wild life park Emma watched apprehensively, but none moved towards the roadway.

A wombat waddled from the edge of the bushland and scuffled back.

Emma wished Simon would stop or at least slow down, but there was something forbidding in his intense concentration as he drove, and she decided this was not the time to ask favours.

He travelled fast along the outback road, and it seemed to Emma he must have known every rise and hollow, every turn in the road.

When they eventually reached Duelgumbah station they lumbered over a cattle grid, and Emma was ordered to open and close gates. The large wooden gate bore the name of the homestead and beneath it the familiar name Delrayo. Emma thought, 'I might have known!' but Simon gave no sign that he noticed her slanted look.

Inside the gate one road pointed towards the

grey-brown earth paddocks, while another turned into an avenue of trees. Simon chose the rough road, heading towards a rocky range of mountains with five rugged peaks thrusting into the sky like the teeth of a rabbit-trap.

'Five tribal elders,' Simon nodded towards them.

'Not very hospitable,' Emma commented.

These were not the green hills of Luradil; they were gnarled outcroppings of rock bursting through scrawny hillsides.

Dust swirled about them as the Land Rover bounced upwards, until Emma felt only the seat belt held her secure. They were high above the plain when they stopped, and she heard small rocks bouncing. She closed her eyes.

'Scared?'

'Certainly not! I'm keeping dust out of my eyes.'

'Put on your sunglasses.'

Simon's own eyes were screened, and there was no sympathy in his voice.

'Look there, over near the horizon, back where we've come from. There's the homestead.'

'You've seen it before?'

'Yes, I've seen it.'

Beside the Land Rover, sheer rock face dropped to the plains. Emma looked down and shuddered.

'Well, I think it's awful,' she said. 'Can we go back now?'

All she could see were paddocks and scattered cattle, and in the distance the homestead and its outbuildings in the centre of an incredible green oasis. Around the homestead several huge white tents had been erected.

'For the barbecue.'

But Simon was more interested in the land immediately below. A river wound across it, with green tree-fringes along its banks. Everywhere else shimmered in heat haze.

Emma asked curiously, 'Is it the way you remember it?'

'Mostly. We'll get going now. I promised to show you the waterfall where the old medicine man is imprisoned. It's at the other end of the hills. You can listen to him chattering, if it amuses you.'

Emma shut her eyes for the descent. She sighed and huddled beside Simon, glancing resentfully at the stern profile, lips thinned and tense as he negotiated the rugged hillside. He took his attention from the tortuous descent only long enough to stare at her grimly, as if daring her to complain.

But when they reached flat ground, and the riverbank, Emma's resentment vanished. The waterfall dropped over the red rocks in a sheet of silver, only breaking into small cascades a few feet above water level.

'There's your medicine man, chattering away full steam. Listen.'

'Poor man, he must be pretty well soaked by now,' commented Emma.

'He's probably found a dry place. There are caves behind the waterfall. I'll show you one day.'

'Bet you can't show me the eel.'

'You'll see his picture on the wall of one of the caves, but not today. We've other things to do.'

'And the girl—the poor maiden. Is her picture there, too?'

'Nope. She's been eliminated.' Simon's face hardened. 'She won't double-cross any more eels.'

'He sounds a nasty type, that eel.' Emma looked everywhere except at Simon. 'Although you seem to be very fond of him. I suppose I'll have to watch you carefully. If you start sprouting wings I'll know you're losing your cool, and I'm in danger of being eliminated.'

'When I lose my cool, sweetheart, you won't have to search for wings. You'll know.'

'I bet I will!' Emma didn't have to be told that Simon Charles was capable of great anger. She didn't want to be reminded.

He made a deliberate attempt to lessen tension.

'Care for a swim, or are you frightened the eel will get you?'

'He wouldn't want me. He only collects beautiful maidens, and nobody's ever called me a beautiful maiden.'

Simon inspected her thoughtfully.

'Haven't they now?' His voice was warm.

In some confusion, she avoided his eyes. She hated the way she blushed when he turned those probing eyes full-strength on her. She said, stammering slightly 'Anyway, I d-don't carry a—a spear. He'd know I w-was the wrong girl.'

He knew he was making her feel awkward. He began unbuttoning the checked shirt he wore, all the time watching her reaction.

'You have your weapons,' he said. If only he would look away from her! He dropped the shirt and began removing the jeans, and Emma resolutely broke the spell that held her, but not before he had seen the deepening flush that stained her neck and cheeks and almost threatened to envelop her whole body.

She wore the flesh-coloured bikini under her yellow shirt and jeans, and with a great show of preoccupation she turned away and stripped off the shirt, finding herself afflicted with unexpected shyness. Tossing down shirt and jeans, she ran quickly into the water. Its coldness made her gasp, and she came up flailing the water. Simon followed more slowly.

Whatever he'd been doing overseas, he'd kept fit. His gymnast's body cut the water arrow-clean, and he swam with slow powerful strokes to the middle of the pool.

'Whatever am I doing out in the middle of no-where with a man like that?' Emma asked herself; and as he struck out for the stronger current she eased herself towards the water's edge. She floated pleasantly in the shallows until Simon splashed out of the pool.

'Okay, pretty maiden,' he ordered, 'out of there and into your jeans. We'll find out what sort of welcome Duelgumbah has for you.'

The homestead was sharing its welcome with a host of people this morning. A constant stream of visitors wandered about the gardens and through the large white tents and down to the holding-yards and a small racetrack.

Emma's eyes widened at the size of the gracious mellow sandstone homestead, its wide verandahs supported by sandstone columns, two extension wings joined to the main building by long breeze-ways.

In contrast to dusty plains, the house and its outbuilding nestled among lawns and spreading trees and gardens bright with flowers. Inside the tents there were trestle tables laden with food; and already the aroma of cooking wafted from the barbecues.

Simon touched her lightly on the shoulder.

'Can you amuse yourself? I'd like to look around.'

Yes, she could amuse herself. Simon disappeared, and she explored the garden, but it was the people on the homestead verandah who interested her most. An elderly man in a wheelchair sat looking at the crowd; a taller-than-average man with white hair, a sad face and drooping shoulders.

Beside him, a woman sat on a wrought iron chair. Although she was not young she sat erect, and she had an air of distinction. Her hair was silver, her dark eyes alert, her face a fine diamond shape with sharply-defined cheekbones. Unlike the man, she paid little attention to the scene around her. Her regard was all for him, her attitude protective.

Farther along the verandah the dark-haired girl from the Festival Dinner and the Winery, with her wilful face, leaned against the wrought-iron railing. She wore beige cords and a chocolate-brown shirt, with a scarlet scarf knotted around her neck. There was something almost disdainful in the way she leaned over the rail watching the crowded gardens.

'Surveying the peasants,' Emma told herself tartly, and then regretted her comment, because the elderly man in the wheelchair looked at her across the wrought-iron railing and inclined his white head and raised a hand in greeting.

Guiltily, Emma waved back. She had been caught staring; and she moved away to watching the swans gliding over a man-made lake.

There had been something attractive about the old man's smile. Emma felt embarrassed, as though he had caught her being unmannerly. She could not know how enchanting she looked, with the cream stetson tilted back on her head, the cloud of soft dark hair waving, slim jeans and yellow shirt with the sleeves rolled up . . .

Despite her natural aversion, Emma managed to work up some interest in the rodeo. She climbed carefully on to a railing fence and unrolled the sleeves of her shirt because already the sun was stinging her skin. She breathed in dust and the smell of overheated beasts and sweating men, and wrinkled her nose.

She pulled the wide-brimmed hat over her forehead, and a voice alongside her said coolly, 'Don't you think you'd be a lot safer down here?'

She snapped, 'Why?' without looking to see who it was.

'Many a beast has tried to shake off his rider by brushing him against the fence. You have to be mighty quick about jumping down if he chooses your part of the rails.'

So this time she turned her head, and there was

the good-looking young man from the Festival Dinner. Emma stared bewildered at what might have been Simon's eyes glinting up at her in unabashed invitation out of a young, clean-shaven face; eyes of clear bright green. She found composure.

'Other people are sitting on fences.'

'Judging by the way you climbed up, I'd say you might be a little less experienced than most people. A frantic animal isn't going to beg your pardon and allow you extra time to jump down just because you're a novice.'

'Oh.' Emma surveyed him doubtfully. 'You're right,' she admitted. 'I don't know anything about it.'

He stood looking at her with an air of supreme confidence. He was good-looking and attractive, and he knew it.

'Carne Delrayo, at your service,' he introduced himself, and Emma wondered why he bothered. There were plenty of attractive girls about. From the looks they cast in his direction they would have come running had he beckoned.

But Carne Delrayo was helping her down from the fence, smiling with practised charm.

He said, 'You're staring at me. I wonder why.'

Emma murmured softly, 'You have unusual eyes.'

He settled the wide-brimmed stetson more firmly on her hair, and Emma added, 'Delrayo! Then you must own—' she spread out her hands—'all this.'

He laughed.

'Not quite. I'm junior. My grandfather and the

rest of the family control most of it, but I have my share.'

As he helped her brush down her jeans he asked, 'Your first visit?'

'To one of these things, yes.'

'And you don't like it much.'

The beautifully shaped mouth smiled at her enchantingly. He was so sure of himself, the bright young man, but charming too. Emma smiled at him.

'No. I think I'll go back to the gardens.'

Only junior, he had said, but he didn't mean it. He had an excellent opinion of himself, and who could blame him? To be part of all this—the elegant homestead, the vineyards, the fat lazy cattle and the fences that seemed to reach for ever.

As though he read her thoughts he said charmingly, 'Did you enjoy your visit to our Winery yesterday? And are you going to tell me your name?'

'Yes, I did enjoy my visit, and my name is Emma.'

He had turned to walk with her towards the homestead; but he stopped then and blocked her way, staring down at her with hard, bright eyes.

'Just Emma. Is that all?'

'Just Emma.'

Somewhere a warning had sounded to Emma. She could think of no good reason, but it seemed the young man had sought her out especially and she didn't understand it. He stared at her for a moment, eyebrows raised, then turned abruptly and led her on.

'You're not a local girl. The locals I know.'

Yes, you would, Emma thought. I bet you would. The pretty ones, anyway; those you considered worthy of your notice.

'And what do you find so intriguing about my eyes, Emma? The colour? Haven't you seen green eyes before?' He was watching her slyly. 'Delrayo eyes! Synonymous with sex, sin and scandal.'

Emma glanced at him obliquely. 'You're all three, I suppose. Sinful, sexy and scandalous.'

He laughed then, a short hard laugh that had no real amusement in it.

'No, Emma, that's my big brother Nicholas you're talking about. Pity you can't meet him, but he found it—er—expedient to leave us a while ago——'

There was a sullen undertone in the beguiling voice, as though he were saying something else, and not the trivial words he spoke. 'Big brother Nick brought scandal to the Delrayos, loads of it. I'm not sure about the sin and sex, but he was a wild boy and did his share of romping, so I guess he covered the spectrum pretty thoroughly.'

His smile was crooked.

'Nobody ever noticed me while Nick was around. He dazzled everyone. I had thought—I really had—that after Nick blotted his copybook I might have been noticed, especially by Grandfather. But no! He doesn't notice anybody now.'

Grandfather! That was probably the old man on the verandah. But he had noticed Emma. From the wheelchair he had looked across the flowers and lawns and raised a frail arm, and Emma was almost sure he'd smiled.

Everybody seems to be noticing me, Emma thought, and found the thought chilling.

'Don't tell me there's a skeleton in the Delrayo cupboards,' she said lightly.

'Not quite a skeleton. Nick's still alive, as far as we know, but heaven knows where.'

He shrugged his shoulders, not looking at her. They passed a clump of pampas grass and he reached out and gathered a plume, twisting it idly in his fingers. Still not looking at her, he said, 'He'll probably turn up one of these days and set the whole town buzzing again.' His voice was bitter.

'You don't sound as if you'd welcome him,' she commented. 'You aren't exactly waving banners for your brother.'

'Don't know anybody who would be, except perhaps a few devoted ladies with long memories.' His smile was lopsided. 'And Grandpa, of course. Poor old Granddad, sitting up there on the verandah in his wheelchair, submerged in regrets.'

'Doesn't he speak at all?' she asked.

'Oh yes, occasional politenesses. But he doesn't really feel any more. All his feelings were for big brother Nicholas; and brother Nick threw them all back in his face. He didn't give a damn.'

Carne screwed the pampas plume viciously in his fingers and flung it away.

'Pay me no attention, Emma. I'm just tired of being Peter Pan—never quite making it to seniority. I thought, with Nick gone—but no, I was still—outshone. That's the word for it. Outshone.'

His mouth twisted.

He said suddenly, 'Do you ride, Emma? Would you like to see the stables?'

'No, thank you. I'm with a friend.'

He made an expression of exaggerated disbelief.

'A friend who leaves you all alone. Bit careless, isn't he?'

'He knows he can trust me.'

He laughed then, green eyes shining the way Simon's eyes gleamed in his relaxing moments.

'Aha! He's complacent. You should do something about that, Emma. Teach him a lesson. Let me know if you need any assistance. We could make him jealous——'

He lifted a hand as he turned away to the stables, and Emma made her way frowningly to the white tents.

She found Simon at the barbecue.

'Finished your snooping?' Her voice was flippant, but she wished she could see more clearly behind the dark glasses. She wanted to compare the two pairs of eyes.

He steered her into the nearest tent.

'Eat well,' he ordered. 'All you'll get tonight is a late hamburger.'

It was late afternoon when they joined the line of vehicles leaving Duelgumbah, and dark when they pulled in at Luradil to buy supper.

They ate by the riverside, sitting on a park bench, watching a full moon rise over the tops of the flowering gums and drop its reflection on to the water.

'I like it here,' Emma said dreamily. 'I don't

think I like rodeos much, Simon. Could we stay here in Luradil?'

'Probably not.'

'Can't you see how lovely it is?'

He said, with undisguised impatience, 'Emma, I found a man today, an old man called Foss. That's not his real name, of course, but I've never known him by any other. He's an old fossicker who wandered around this district all his life. I think he's going to tell me something—I've arranged to meet him tomorrow. And after that, who knows? We may stay, we may leave.'

'You won't find anywhere better than this.'

'There are places.'

'Look at the moon on the river. It's just like my ring.' Emma held up her left hand, fingers outspread. 'See? The pearl in the centre and those golden ripples around it.'

Simon grinned.

'Thought you didn't go in for poetry. Now who's romancing?'

'I'm not.'

She got down from the seat and sat, chin resting on her hands, watching the moon on the water. Stealthily the man picked up a stone and threw it with deadly accuracy into the river. It shattered the moon's reflection, breaking it into a flurry of ripples.

'What's happened to your fancies now?'

He would have tossed another stone, but as he reached for it, Emma pushed it away with her foot.

'Leave it alone. You're destructive. Anyhow, the

moon will come back, you'll see. It'll be back just as soon as you get tired of chasing it away. You can't beat nature.'

He turned to look at her, oval face white-pearl in the moonlight, a golden beam glancing off soft brown hair, the pure young profile as she leaned forward, tracing the ripples on the water.

He lifted his head sharply then, staring at her, standing suddenly still as though he held his breath. When he spoke his voice was strained.

'No,' he agreed, 'you're right, young lady. You can't beat nature.' Then he stooped and lifted her with his powerful arms. 'Time to go.'

Emma fumed at him, 'I don't want to go! I'm not ready yet.'

She imagined she saw the glimmering of a faint smile.

'That's right, Emma, you aren't ready yet.'

She broke away to sit again, but he grasped her roughly.

'Didn't you hear? It's time to go.'

He steered her determinedly ahead of him. 'Get moving,' he ordered, and his voice had a husky timbre she had not heard in it before. It made her want to turn her head and look at him as he walked behind her. But when she turned, his face was hidden in the shadows of a lacy-leafed jacaranda tree.

CHAPTER SEVEN

AFTERWARDS Emma wondered why she hadn't the slightest premonition of disaster as she followed Simon to the Land Rover. If her senses had been alert she must surely have felt the vibrations of danger. They always came whenever she got herself comfortable. Just when she imagined she'd found a permanent home with Willie and his friends; just when her mother had seemed to brighten and strengthen. Happiness had always been for her the forerunner of disaster. So why not now?

But the night was so calm as they turned into the driveway between the peppertrees. Valerie stood on the verandah as they drove in. Emma yawned and stretched and went to talk to Val while Simon opened the caravan.

'Enjoy the rodeo?'

Emma pulled a little face.

'It was all right, I suppose. Did you have another busy day at the Winery?'

'Did we ever? Come inside when you've freshened up, and tell us about Duelgumbah.' Val's glance travelled affectionately over Emma's rumpled hair and sleepy face. 'That's if you'd rather not go to bed. I'll make a pot of tea.'

'Thanks, Valerie, I'd love to. I'll tell Simon.'

Emma was still smiling as she stepped into the

caravan; then suddenly all the pleasure of the evening was gone.

Simon stood grimly between the bed and the table, and all around him groceries and provisions lay strewn on the floor, and heaps of disarranged clothing had been flung everywhere. Every cupboard emptied; even the storage space under the bed had been rifled; it hung half open, a fishing-rod bent between two rubber boots.

Emma whispered, 'Who would do such a thing? Children?'

'No, this isn't vandals' work. Your housekeeping money is still here. It's untouched. Thank God I had my wallet with me, and all my papers. And you, Emma—did you leave any identifying papers?'

'For heaven's sake, who would want to identify me?'

His voice grated. '*Did* you?'

Emma felt the wallet in her pocket and shook her head dumbly.

Simon cleared a space on the seat and sat down heavily.

'That's it, then,' he said. 'Somebody knows I'm here.'

She wasn't all that surprised. Even among the hundreds of tourists the lanky man with the luxuriant beard remained distinguished by something no one else had; an air of distinction, of vigour and of pride. Of course he'd be recognised. He always would be. You didn't disguise a mountain by draping a cloud around its summit . . .

It was comical, if you kept thinking about it, but

she wouldn't dare say so to Simon. There wasn't anything constructive she could say to him now.

He made no attempt to clean up the mess, and when Emma began uneasily sorting groceries he stopped her.

'Leave it.'

'It h-has to be done,' she answered. 'V-Valerie and Len invited us in for a drink, and I said we'd go.'

He shot her a glance from under taut brows.

'Emma, that's your first stammer for a while. Don't get upset, for God's sake.'

'I'm n-not. But the man at the Winery—he recognised you. And he was afraid.'

He nodded agreement.

'Douglas Delrayo,' he agreed. 'My dear uncle. And if Douglas, I suppose there'd be others. Probably I expected a bit much, but I thought—five years—I must have changed.'

Not enough, Emma amended silently.

He paced the caravan, and because it was so small he could only take four steps each way; and Emma saw that he was confined and frustrated. He stopped pacing and stared at her, frowning.

Emma said, 'Don't w-worry about me. I'll survive.'

'Sit down.' Simon shoved a heap of clothing on to the floor. 'You have to know what it's about, Emma, so you can decide. Whether you prefer to go along with me, or leave. It's not such a big thing, not to anybody else but me and one other person whose identity I'm not sure of. And I don't think it involves any danger to you. But if you want out, you can say so. And you can never be sure of what people will do—how they'll react.'

Emma sat listening carefully, because Simon wasn't in a mood to say anything twice. He spoke quickly and fiercely, and she had to catch it all, every syllable, if she was to understand.

He said, 'It happened five—nearly six—years ago. I was twenty-five, finished university, back from a quick trip overseas to study wine-making in Italy and France. My twenty-sixth birthday present from my grandfather was a red Porsche car. I took my place on the board of the Winery and was ready to study management of Duelgumbah. My grandfather owns several cattle stations, but this was the one I wanted. I thought I had everything.'

He settled on the edge of the bed, the strong hands with their long tanned fingers hanging idly between his knees.

'Then one night I drove to the Winery—*this* Winery in *this* valley—and left the Porsche in the car park. There were rumours of theft; stories of boats moving along the river at night. It was worth a check.'

He stopped, remembering. Emma saw the wince of pain that came with the memory.

'You're a Delrayo, then. I thought so.'

His head lifted. 'That's right.'

'Then there never was a Simon Charles.'

He managed a crooked smile.

'My name is Nicholas Simon Charles Delrayo.'

'All that much?'

'All that. And the night it happened, I spent several hours walking along the river banks and through the vineyard. I found nothing—a couple of genuine fishermen in a small boat; that was all. It was a peaceful night, black with no moon, but very pleasant. I remember sitting by the river. Maybe I stayed too long; but I wanted to be sure there were no intruders.'

He shook himself back into the present.

'I wandered back to the car park, and was just approaching my car when the police arrived. They told me my Porsche had been involved in a hit-and-run accident in the main street of Luradil. I laughed at them. My car hadn't moved, I said. I would have seen the headlights, or heard the motor.

'But I was wrong. The front mudguard was crumpled, the bumper bar damaged. I hadn't noticed it in the dark.'

He made a sound, half sigh, half pain. Emma wanted to tell him to stop, but she doubted whether he would have heard. 'My car had hit, and killed, a crippled man in a wheelchair, a man already paralysed after a previous accident. He was well known in the district. He'd been drinking heavily, he usually did in the evenings, and he'd wheeled himself out suddenly from between parked cars.'

'Could somebody have taken your car?' she asked.

'Easily. In a town like Luradil, you trust everybody. I left the keys in the ignition—I always did.'

'And somebody saw it happen.'

'Several people saw the car. The only real witness was an eighteen-year-old named Neville Bearsden, the son of another station owner. He told the police at first I was driving.'

'How could he?'

'At first he insisted he was certain, but later he admitted he could have been wrong. It could have been a man who looked like me. Other people saw the car. In ordinary circumstances it might have been called an unfortunate, unavoidable accident—the wheelchair had lurched out so suddenly. But my car was speeding, and there was the hit-and-run thing. That was worst of all.'

'It definitely was your car?'

Simon's smile twisted.

'Mine was the only one of its kind in the district. And of course there was the damage. And Neville saying he thought I was driving. Although he watered down his evidence later.'

'You went to prison?'

The same twisted smile.

'No. I had a good lawyer, the best my grandfather's money could provide. And Neville proved an unrealiable witness. He wavered. Fortunately I'd spoken to the two blokes in the boat. I suppose that helped, although they weren't exactly certain about the time. But why on earth didn't the person who pinched my car and drove it into Luradil come out into the open? What sort of mongrel lets another man take his punishment?'

Simon's hands clenched. Emma wanted to hold them, but she stayed stiffly in her seat. He wasn't thinking about her now. He was turning back several years.

'Anyway, I was absolved. But most people believed it was me. There was—unpleasantness. My grandfather had suffered a massive stroke only a few weeks before. He was a sensitive man. My grandmother suggested I go abroad again.

'So that's what happened. I was despatched overseas to resume my study of vineyards and wine-making. To let things simmer down. There were anonymous letters—phone calls—unpleasant incidents. Apparently nobody was too willing to believe in the phantom joyrider who stole my car.'

'Your parents?'

'Both died in a plane crash when we were children. My grandparents reared us—my young brother Carne, and myself. We led very happy lives. Then suddenly—wham! All of it gone in one night's dirty work.'

'Do you have a sister? The dark girl——'

'Leitha? No, she's Uncle Doug's daughter. Douglas is my father's brother.'

'Oh. I'm sorry I interrupted. What's the rest of the story?'

'By the end of twelve months I was ready to come home, but Grandmother sent me another letter, suggesting I prolong my so-called holiday. My grandfather's health was failing; there were still strong feelings in the town; he was so frail now that the slightest distress could have disastrous effects. She believed I must make my own decision. But of course she said, and I quote, "in your grandfather's interests I suggest you stay longer" . . .'

He shrugged, a bitter shrug.

'So I stayed away another four years. I worked in vineyards; acquired a financial interest in several. I suppose I might have stayed even longer, but I met a friend in California, where I studied wine-making. And he mentioned the old man, Foss; he'd been boasting in the pub one night, making mysterious remarks about the accident and something he knew that nobody else did. So I decided that if I could come home unrecognised, and get hold of old Foss, and maybe talk some more to young Neville, perhaps I could set the matter straight. Somebody knows what happened. The person who drove my car knows. They won't forget.'

'Won't your family know you're here? By your letters?'

'All mail goes through my accountant these last few years. I still receive dividends from the Delrayo Winery and other properties, all through the accountant. We don't indulge in family correspondence often. I don't have the urge.'

'You should have made them believe you were innocent.'

His lips were a bitter line.

'They ought to have known.'

'And that's all?' asked Emma.

'There are a few other things. Profits from the Delrayo Winery have been consistently falling. The reason given my accountant was the need to extend acreage, to purchase mechanical harvesters, stainless steel fermentation tanks, and a drop in sales. Yet Len says business is thriving, crops good, and markets expanding. So why?'

'And you've come to Luradil to ask your questions. You found the old man, didn't you? And don't you think somebody is going to stop you asking questions?'

'Yes to both, obviously. Old Foss was at the rodeo, but didn't want to talk to me there. He'll see me at his property tomorrow morning. Now there's a very interesting phenomenon.'

'Why?' she asked.

'Old Foss never had a bank account to bless himself with. Just roamed around the rivers, panning for gold, fossicking for bits of emerald or jasper or whatever he could find. Doing a bit of digging here and there; shooting other people's sheep when he got hungry, pinching whatever he could find. And suddenly, bingo! he's a man of property. Not a lot, but enough. Nice little bit of land the other side of Luradil, with a house. They say he doesn't fossick any more. I thought I'd ask him why, tomorrow morning.'

He stood up with a lithe, deliberate movement. 'I'm sure of one thing; whoever "borrowed" my car and killed that poor devil in the wheelchair is still around. Why else would anybody bother to search the van? So, Emma, although I don't think you're in danger, you've a decision to make.'

'I have?'

He gestured at the scattered clothes and provisions. 'I invited you on this excursion as a bit of extra camouflage for me. It hasn't stuck, has it?'

'Nobody will hurt me,' she said carelessly.

'I don't believe they will. I don't believe they'll hurt me either. I think somebody wanted to make sure who I was, that's all. But if you'd like to go, Emma, you won't leave penniless. I owe you something—It won't take all that long to drive you back to the coast.'

'Trying to get rid of me?'

She thought his expression looked strained through the tan. There were grim lines around his mouth, and he was tired. She decided swiftly.

'I'll stay.'

'You're sure, Emma? Don't make promises you can't keep.'

Emma answered furiously, 'I can keep——'

'If you stay with me,' he was warning, 'I have to be able to rely on you.'

Her voice was truculent.

'You pay me, don't you? I'll earn the money.'

'Ah, yes, the money,' he said.

As though for one fleeting instant he might have forgotten they had a deal between them; as though he might have been talking man-to-woman, friend to friend. The cool mouth tightened again, the eyes bleaker.

'All right, Emma, you've got yourself a bargain. You look pretty and cook meals, and I'll try not to involve you in my stirring.'

He stood up suddenly and began tidying, and Emma said to herself, You wouldn't really want to talk man-woman to me. Or friend to friend. Not to a little beach girl you picked up from the water one afternoon when you didn't have anything better to do.

She said, 'Leave the clothes on the bed. I'll fix them later. Why don't we go and have supper with Len and Val? We can clear up when we come home.'

As he stood aside to let her go through the doorway a phantom smile softened the grimness.

'So it's "home" already, is it?'

Simon seemed content to listen while Len talked, and Emma and Valerie shared their pot of tea. Emma thought the search of the caravan had jolted him.

As they walked back to the caravan later she said wistfully, 'I suppose you couldn't just forget it, could you? I mean, it's past, isn't it? Wouldn't you like to enjoy the last few days of the festival?'

But he didn't agree. 'You can enjoy yourself tomorrow while I go and talk to old Foss. You'll probably have to do more shopping. I see they've burst open our bag of flour and broken one of our jamjars.'

When the clearing-up was finished he looked at her doubtfully.

'Emma, you're sure you want to stay with me?'

'Why? Do you want your ring back?'

He froze then.

'Do you want to give it back to me?'

'I've grown accustomed to it.' Her voice was gruff. 'But I know it's valuable. And I'm n-not much use to you any more, am I?'

He studied her without smiling.

'You can still cook, can't you?'

'Yes, I can still do that.'

'That'll do, then. I don't know how long I'll be with old Foss tomorrow. You can lunch in town if you like. And how about producing something special for dinner?'

'Such as?'

'Surprise me.'

Emma wished he had given the shadow of a smile, anything to relieve the gloom, but he hadn't smiled since he'd discovered the ransacked caravan, and he wasn't smiling now.

After he closed the door, Emma sat twisting the ring on her finger. Once again she had been offered a chance to break away, and not taken it. She had made a decision that surprised herself.

She put the ring away for safety, and sat trying to decide what she would cook tomorrow. She heard Simon moving in the annexe, then silence, as though he had settled down for the night. She had wanted so desperately to relieve the tension.

She crept to the door and opened it just far enough to put her head around the opening.

'What do you say to chicken with pineapple? Followed by chocolate mousse? It's a Wilson special.'

She heard a low grunt, then the soft thud as a piece of rolled-up clothing hit the door.

'Go to sleep.'

The order was gruff, but there was a suspicion of amusement beneath, and a suspicion was better than nothing, Emma told herself. She pulled on the shirt with its scarlet flowers and climbed into bed.

CHAPTER EIGHT

SIMON did not travel smiling into Luradil next morning. He went sternly, the implacable jaw outthrust, his expression preoccupied as he swung the Land Rover to a stop outside the post office for Emma to get out.

He did not glance back after he left her. That made Emma feel lonely. So when she completed her shopping and stacked it in the caravan, she put on the yellow silk dress and brushed her hair, then wandered back to the main street, to the colours, and the sounds of music.

There were several restaurants, as well as two hotels and a Chinese café. Emma hovered outside the hotel, trying to decide where to eat, when a firm hand grasped her elbow and Carne Delrayo bent his head and smiled at her and said, 'Hello. Abandoned again?'

He added, 'I'd choose the restaurant across the road if I were you. No empty tables in the Chinese Dragon. I just looked in.'

Emma said steadily, 'I can wait.'

'Please don't. I may as well confess I came into Luradil hoping I'd find you. I knew it wouldn't be difficult.'

'How did you know that?'

His grin was impertinent and at the same time attractive.

'Emma, you'd never get lost in a crowd. I'd find you anywhere.'

The flowery compliment came too easily. Emma felt uncomfortably sure there was more to their meeting than accident. There were prettier girls all around, dozens of them. He was nervous, too. It showed under the smooth charm, the determined brilliance of his smiling, the forceful way he took her elbow as if determined not to let her go. He was trying so hard to impress.

'That escort of yours, he's not very attentive, is he?'

'Simon is busy,' Emma fenced steadily.

'I expect he is.' Carne spread his hands in an extravagant gesture of persuasion. 'But surely not too busy to pay attention to such an attractive lady-friend. He's a bit careless, it seems to me.'

His eyes were shrewd, searching.

'You *are* his girl-friend, aren't you?'

He glanced at the pearl ring. Emma answered quickly, 'Of course I am.'

'Well, if he leaves you alone at the festival, he can't complain if I offer you lunch. You don't want to spend the day alone, do you?'

No, she didn't. She honestly didn't. Emma suppressed her suspicion and allowed herself to be led into the restaurant. Even if she hadn't known Carne was a Delrayo she would soon have realised he was someone of importance. They were ushered to the best available table, waited on deferentially, the manageress standing by discreetly in case they required additional service. Carne Delrayo was accustomed to attention. Other diners went out of their way to greet him. He was a privileged person and a popular one.

He asked, 'Where do you come from, Emma?'

Emma shrugged carelessly. 'Nowhere special.'

He grinned engagingly.

'All right, don't tell me. Keep your dark secrets. If I want to find out, I'll go back and follow the trail of broken hearts.'

Emma laughed. 'Some trail!'

'Don't tell me you haven't left countless fractured male egos behind you?'

She didn't realise where he was leading her. She replied impulsively, 'I've led an uneventful life, looking after my invalid mother until she died. Then I came to New South Wales, to the Sapphire Coast, to join my brother. So I didn't have time to b-break any hearts.'

Those watchful green eyes should have warned her.

'You haven't known the ring-giving gallant very long, then? You *did* say fiancé——?'

Almost, Emma fell into the trap. The words trembled in her throat, ready to come out: 'Oh no, we've only just met'—But she felt the vibrations of mistrust in time.

She moistened her lips and swallowed.

'Of course w-we're engaged. If you're talking about Simon.'

'Tall, rather fearsome-looking gent, skulking behind dark beard and heavy sunglasses.' He was pretending to tease, but his eyes stayed watchful. Concentrating, as though willing her to be truthful . . .

Emma stared at him dumbly. How could she say 'Simon and I will be married any day now,' when she knew it wasn't true? She fumbled with a spoon and finally said in a small voice, 'You ask a lot of questions, don't you?'

'Yes, I do, Emma my love. And I haven't finished yet. I'll probably think of more before this meal is over. Meantime, relax. Let's enjoy ourselves.'

It wasn't long before Emma found herself enjoying his youthful efforts to charm. She didn't believe him—oh, never—but it was exciting to be told that her hair was the most exciting thing he had ever seen, her eyes the dreamiest and most enchanting——

'Tell me more. You might say something I can believe in a minute.'

Her eyes were dancing with laughter when Carne looked over her shoulder and exclaimed, 'Well, look who's here!' and she turned, suddenly apprehensive, expecting Simon.

It was the girl from the Winery, the elegant young girl with the black hair so like Carne's, and the young, cruel mouth. Today she wore a simple dress in purple with an extravagant collection of gold chains around her neck and slim wrists.

She said without looking at Emma, 'Carne, whatever are you doing here among the tourists?' and her voice was cutting-cool.

'Dining, my dear Leitha. That's what I'm doing, as you see.'

He stood and pulled out a chair for the girl as he explained, 'This is my cousin Leitha. And this is

Emma.' The girl barely nodded. Her attention remained reserved for Carne.

'I'll join you for a drink. Wine, not coffee. And afterwards you can come shopping with me.'

Leitha sat fastidiously sipping her drink while they finished lunch. Every time she spoke, it seemed to Emma's sensitive ear, she went out of her way to make Emma feel uncomfortable. I might be the invisible woman, Emma found herself thinking. Leitha's expensive perfume floated across the table in waves of exquisite scent as she waved her hands. She acted with vital, supercilious grace that would have left Emma tongue-tied had she not become angry.

They were sipping coffee when Leitha refused a second glass of wine. She put her empty glass on the table and beckoned Carne imperiously.

'We'll have to move,' she commanded. 'You know how long it takes to buy things with all these tourists around.'

Emma said perversely, 'I'd like another cup of coffee, please,' and saw the glimmer of a smile flicker over Carne's face. He called the waitress, and when Emma's coffee was poured they sat politely while she finished it. It was hot, and she could not hurry over it.

Carne was enjoying the situation; he understood her gesture of independence and the embarrassment of the hot coffee. He waited until her cup was empty and then asked politely, 'All finished? Or would you like another cup?'

The ghost of laughter lingered in the green Delrayo eyes while she shook her head.

'Wine, perhaps?'

The other girl pushed back her chair imperiously.

'Oh, come *on*,' she ordered, and flounced to the door.

Outside on the footpath the crowds seemed to have increased. The girl directed Carne with an inclination of her sleek head.

'I'm going to buy a saddle blanket. Dad says there are some worth looking at in the Arcade. Come and help me choose.'

She didn't bother to say goodbye to Emma but swept away, threading her regal way among the 'tourists'. Carne offered Emma a tentative smile.

'We'll meet again.'

'Perhaps. Thank you for the lunch.'

'We'll repeat the excursion. I'll find you.' Emma watched him stride after the other girl with a pang of loneliness. He had tried so cleverly to entertain her, and despite misgivings she had to admit she had basked in the warmth of his attention. She sighed and looked around her.

Across the street, Simon stood very still, under the shelter of an orange-flowered gumtree. Emma wondered how long he had stood there, watching, and whether he had seen the three of them emerge from the restaurant. He must have seen them together, for she could feel his disapproval as clearly as if he had spoken it.

To her annoyance Emma felt guilty. Simon strode across the street, dodging cars, and coming to a standstill on the footpath beside her, unsmiling.

She said defensively, 'Don't worry, I haven't betrayed you. You needn't go on about black holes in the sky and things like that. We met accidentally.'

He stood there, disbelieving. Emma shut her lips crossly, and when she finally spoke her voice was sharp.

'I know he's your brother, and I was very careful. I didn't tell him anything.'

As they walked to the car park he said cynically, 'Are you telling me he didn't ask?'

Emma said evasively, 'We had the usual polite conversation, that's all.'

It wasn't all, and she was uncomfortably aware of it. Carne Delrayo would have been delighted to accept any scrap of information he could have wheedled out of her. He had asked more than his share of questions. But Simon's forbidding expression deterred her from making confessions.

She protested weakly, almost running to keep pace with his angry strides, 'At least he offered some polite conversation. That's more than you bother to do. We met at the rodeo yesterday, and then we met in town, accidentally.'

'And the girl, Leitha, did you meet her at the rodeo, too?'

'No, but I saw her at the Festival Dinner. She's your cousin, isn't she? How old is she, or don't you trust me enough to tell me?'

He softened then; perhaps her barb about his lack of conversation had hit home.

'Leitha must be about nineteen or twenty, I should think. Her mother's an Englishwoman, I think she's in London now, visiting relatives, from what Len says.' He quirked an eyebrow at her ironically. 'Her father is the gentleman you had all those suspicions about. Remember?'

'You have a large family,' Emma said at last.

His smile was derisive.

'You think that's good?'

'Yes, I do. I think you're lucky. I don't have anybody. Only Willie. There's no one else.'

They had reached the Land Rover, and Simon stopped before opening the door, looking down at her with a small frown between his eyes.

'Don't tell me you're getting softhearted about your underhanded brother?'

Emma said sadly, 'He's my brother. I do feel responsible. Somebody ought to care about him.'

He sighed, the first time she had ever heard him despondent, rather than angry. His eyes were tired.

'We all have our problems. I forgot yours, being so involved with my own. Selfish of me. What would you like me to do, Emma?'

She said in a small voice, 'I don't know. I just feel—not *you*, but *me*—that I ought to be doing something.'

'I'll make a couple of telephone calls if it makes you feel better. Those kids are probably cooling their heels, waiting to come before the court. There used to be a good solicitor up that way; I imagine he's still around. I'll see what I can do. Your dear brother and his mates might escape with a bond and a stiff fine, since it's their first offence. Their first detected offence, that is,' he added tartly.

Emma hunched her shoulders, and Simon bent

to open the door, and touched her lightly, ruffling her hair with the palm of his hand.

'Don't worry. We might rescue your brother from the mess he's got himself into. Will that satisfy you?'

Emma nodded glumly.

'You think he's bad, don't you?'

'What's your verdict?'

'I d-don't think he's bad, only foolish.'

'Emma,' his voice was gentler, 'you're stammering——'

'I know.' She gave him a crooked smile. 'B-but I'm almost cured.'

'So I'd noticed. And I'm sorry I jumped at you, Emma; but I've had a big disappointment, and I took out my frustration on you.'

'Doesn't your old man know anything?'

Simon's mouth twisted ruefully.

'Chances are, I think, that he knows a lot. Because he's disappeared. Packed his belongings and taken himself far, far away. I can't find anybody who'll tell me where, except that he left last night. He, or somebody assisting him, has performed an instant disappearing act. I'd say he had help. Instant disappearance is difficult to achieve without help.'

'What will you do now?' she asked.

'I don't know, Emma. But I won't give up.'

As she got into the Land Rover, Emma wished she didn't feel so defensive. She had been enjoying herself lunching with Carne while Simon faced disappointment. She knew Simon didn't like it.

She found herself wondering how old Carne

would have been at the time of the accident. He looked twenty-three or four now . . . so he might have been seventeen or eighteen . . . old enough to go for a stolen joyride in his brother's car . . .

'The behaviour of one's brother,' Simon had told her once, 'is not always brotherly . . .'

Horrified, Emma pushed the idea away. What a disaster it would be for Simon if the culprit turned out to be a member of his own family. If not Carne, what about his uncle, Douglas Delrayo? Now, there was a worried man.

Deep in thought, Emma hardly noticed the sumptuous black Daimler parked outside Len's house, but Simon saw it. Emma heard his sharp intake of breath, felt his sudden stiffening.

She asked, puzzled, 'Important visitors for Len and Valerie?'

But as they alighted from the Land Rover Simon grasped her arm and would have hustled her into the caravan had not Valerie come out on to the verandah, beckoning.

'Simon! Somebody here to see you.'

Simon followed Valerie inside reluctantly, taking Emma with him. Inside the house, Emma found the silver-haired woman who had been sitting on the homestead verandah at Duelgumbah. She sat in a chair near the window. Her eyes strained over Len's shoulder as she talked to him, as if she waited with great expectation for the man who came through the doorway.

Yet when Simon came in, she said nothing. She wanted so much to speak, but it was Simon who had to break the long, cool silence.

He said, 'Grandmother,' and the chill in his voice was like the wind in winter. The woman stood up, calming herself as if she were quite used to exercising control.

'It *is* you, Nick. Why haven't you been to see us?'

'I had important things to do, Grandmother.' He motioned her to sit down, without tenderness, as though her emotion moved him not at all. Her clear blue eyes devoured him, as if she tried to penetrate through the mask of curly black hair and heavy beard, seeking familiar features.

Valerie and Len left the room, and Emma wanted to follow, but Simon caught her hand and presented her to the older woman with studied formality.

'Grandmother, this is my fiancée, Emma Wilson. Emma, my grandmother.'

She looked so calm, now, the woman in the chair; but as Emma touched her hand she felt it trembling; but Simon appeared not to notice.

'How did you know I was here?'

'Philip—your grandfather—he was so sure he saw you at the homestead. We told him no, but he was positive, although it was only a glimpse. Then Carne said something strange last night, so I had enquiries made—and I decided to ask one of the men to drive me, so that I could judge for myself.'

Simon asked, 'What do you want?' as if he spoke to a stranger.

'We want to—to welcome you home. Nick, your grandfather longs to talk to you. He sent me. I came to ask you—to come home, if you will.'

It seemed to Emma that Simon might have relented a little, although he gave no sign of it. He sat facing his grandmother, and when he spoke his voice was bitter.

'You needn't have driven all this way. You could have sent a note, like you did last time.'

'Nick.' The sensitive hands, heavily and expensively ringed, moved in protest. 'I know my letter hurt you. I wish there had been someone else to write it. But we were all so distressed about your grandfather. We had to choose——'

'And you made your choice. You told me to stay away.'

'What else could I have done?'

'Nothing, of course.'

'I do have something special to ask you, Nicholas. Douglas is giving an engagement party for Leitha and Neville tomorrow night, at Duelgumbah. We are all hoping—praying—that you and Emma will come. Perhaps if you talked with us——'

Simon made a gesture of negation.

'Later, perhaps.'

'I'm sorry. We'd hoped—all of us——' Irene Delrayo managed a warm clear smile for Emma. 'Poor Neville! He's been proposing to Leitha for so many years I don't think any of us expected anything to come of it. Ever since schooldays. Before'—her voice stumbled—'before Nick went away. Douglas tells me Leitha made up her mind only yesterday. She's not quite twenty yet, I would have imagined Douglas might have preferred them to wait, but he seems to be encouraging it. They're anxious to marry as soon as they can, then they're off to New Zealand for a honeymoon.'

'Sudden as that, is it?' Simon's voice was abrupt.

'Yes. But Leitha always was unpredictable, even as a child. Remember how she led Neville on? I don't think he's ever looked at another girl since the first time he saw Leitha.'

Unexpectedly, Simon asked, 'What time do you want us to arrive?' and she made a quick, delighted movement of her hands, so that the rings glittered. The bright blue eyes were alight with pleasure.

'Nick—oh, I'm so pleased! Could you come in the afternoon, both of you? And Nick, if you could find time to talk to your grandfather. He thinks about you all the time. And you'll stay overnight—you must.' Her voice pleaded. 'You will, won't you?'

'All right. Have you had lunch, Grandmother?'

'Yes, thank you, Nicholas. I mustn't stay, it's such a long drive home.'

When I'm an old lady, Emma thought—if I ever am—I hope I'm valiant, like Irene Delrayo. It was the first time she had ever been truly angry with Simon. Only when she remembered the nightmares, and the calling in the night, could Emma begin to understand how Simon remained so unresponsive.

She said impulsively, 'Would you like to see our caravan?'

'Yes, I would—another time. But my driver is waiting. Thank you, Emma.'

Irene Delrayo had grace and charm. She won Emma with the vibrancy of her spirit and her careful control of the sadness that only showed itself in glimpses when she looked at Simon.

Simon escorted her to the car and when he returned Emma said, 'You're an unforgiving person.'

'Wouldn't you be?'

But inside the caravan he said with unexpected gentleness, 'Emma, would you like more finery for the party?'

'No, thank you. My white dress will do.'

CHAPTER NINE

EMMA wasn't so confident about the white chiffon as they sat around the elegant dining table at Duelgumbah. She had thought the Festival Dinner a glittering occasion; it was nothing compared with the sparkle and glamour of Leitha's engagement party.

Surreptitiously, Emma studied the Delrayo family and their guests. Everybody called Simon 'Nicholas', which she found confusing. It shook her confidence.

Philip Delrayo, the man in the wheelchair, took trouble to be kind to her, but his delight was centred on the tall bearded grandson who had finally come home. Emma noticed his left hand tremble as he poured wine. His right arm appeared useless, and he was so very frail, pale skin tight-stretched over face and fingers, the long lean frame wasted.

His eyes were bright and green, like Simon's; yet he had a wistful sadness in them, as though he had lost resolution. If he had ever been as powerful as Simon, the signs of it were gone. Yet the resemblance remained. Emma looked at the frail old man and thought, 'Simon' . . . and somebody said 'Nicholas' . . . and she stared, bewildered and unhappy, at the tablecloth, wishing she were anywhere else but here.

Leitha did her best to add to Emma's discomfort. She made no attempt to hide her hostility. Simon's fiancée wasn't worth noticing, her offhand greeting made that very plain. The adoring young man still showered her with his fervent attention, only tonight his actions were proprietorial. Emma thought, She'll do what she likes with him; and it might have been amusing, except that somewhere among this glittering sophisticated group of people Simon was being swallowed up, and she would be bereft and confused and on her own again.

After dinner, Leitha moved quickly to Simon's side. She ignored Emma.

'Uncle Nick, how sweet of you to come to my party!' Her voice was honey-sweet and very clear. 'You know Carolyn will be here later? Somebody must have told you.'

She wanted Emma to hear. Her sharp face was alive with mischief and malice.

'Carolyn wants to talk to you. I think she's only coming, because you're here. But perhaps you won't care to see your ex-fiancée now.' She swept Emma with a look, of such concentrated dislike that Emma shivered. 'You've other interests now, Uncle Nick, haven't you?'

Leitha swept triumphantly away and Simon muttered, 'Spoilt brat!' but Emma saw that he was irresolute, as though he had been taken by surprise and wasn't quite sure how to react.

She wanted to ask, 'Who is Carolyn?' but stayed quiet. She was going to find out soon enough, wasn't she? In her mind a memory stirred . . . Simon in nightmare, reaching out for her, muttering, 'Caro . . . Caro . . .' as though he hungered.

When Carolyn arrived, exquisite in an aura of elegance and composure and expensive perfume, Emma saw that it was the glamorous blonde from the Festival Dinner; and now she was more alluring than ever. She wore a soft pink Grecian drape, leaving one perfect shoulder exposed and her exciting figure provocatively outlined. She smothered Simon with extravagant welcome, intimately curving slender white arms around his bulky shoulders.

He extricated himself deliberately, though not too quickly, Emma noted. His eyes were quizzical, the sensuous mouth softened, half amused.

He murmured, 'Caro, this is Emma. We're engaged.' And Emma's heart did a slow spiral, because this must be the most beautiful woman she had ever seen. What a way to die, she mused achingly; smiling politely while all your silly dreams scuttled away like leaves in winter wind . . . smiling through stiff lips . . . pretending you didn't care.

Carolyn purred, 'Nicholas! Always the unexpected. So you're going to be married!' She flicked Emma's finger lightly, with its gleaming pearl. 'Not the diamond, Nick?'

He did not answer; he stood there dark and splendid and secret in his formal clothes; and Carolyn slid one beautifully-manicured hand around his wrist.

'Nick, I have something to show you. You don't mind, Emma, do you? I want to borrow him.'

It was Carne who rescued Emma. He took her on to the dance floor, and because her brother and his friends had taught her disco dancing, she found herself dancing expertly with Carne. So she had something to be grateful to Willie for, after all; that she did not become a wallflower at this grand celebration; that she was not left alone and desolate and out of place in this house of gaily chattering strangers. Because Simon had disappeared, and the beautiful blonde was missing, too.

Once, a long time later, Emma saw them both on the dance floor. Simon, who had announced so vehemently that he did not dance, moved on to the floor with the most beautiful woman Emma had ever seen, and he and she moved gracefully together.

Emma felt humiliated. She pressed herself behind the shadowed palms on the terrace, waiting for Carne to bring her a promised cool drink. But Leitha found her.

Leitha said, with barbed politeness, nodding towards Simon and Carolyn, 'They make a perfect couple, don't they? Of course, they always did.' Her mouth was sullen, as if the evening had tired her. 'They were engaged, you know. Only Carolyn gave him back his ring when he got into trouble. I expect you know about it.'

Emma gathered her dignity and managed a bright smile.

'Naturally I've heard.'

The other girl's eyes were insolent. 'I'd take him away from here, if I were you. Get him out of this as fast as you can, back on the beaches or wherever he picked you up.'

Emma argued fiercely, 'He didn't——'

'Oh, come now. He certainly didn't meet you in his usual social whirl. He's really shaken himself free of the family, hasn't he? Didn't even give you the Delrayo diamond to pledge his troth? Just that pearl thing——'

'Not the diamond, Nick?' Carolyn had murmured. As if she read Emma's thoughts Leitha added spitefully, 'It was Nick's mother's ring. Carolyn returned it when she broke the engagement, but I bet she wouldn't mind having it back now her marriage has broken up. Only lasted two years; he wasn't ambitious enough for Carolyn. Perhaps she's doing a re-think about the diamond. I'd move on, if I were you.'

Over Leitha's shoulder, Emma saw the anxious face of Douglas Delrayo following his daughter's movements. Desperate eyes. Had he sent her to try and prod Emma into dragging Simon away?

Emma said as calmly as she could manage, 'He'll go when he wants to go.'

Leitha gave a light superficial laugh as she walked away, as if she didn't care a damn. 'Please yourself. Only you've a lot to lose, haven't you?'

Emma didn't see her again that night. But later she saw Douglas Delrayo again, silent and watching, while Simon stood beside his grandfather's wheelchair, talking. She saw the jawbone strained hard against his skin, the tension in his upthrust head as he strained to watch.

Emma had only a few glimpses of Simon after that. She danced with Carne, smiling mechanically, her heart reminding her, refusing to forget the 'Caro . . . Caro' of Simon's grief in the night. The girl he had chosen to marry. The girl who had worn the diamond, not the pearl.

It delighted Carne that he and Emma attracted so much attention on the dance floor. It was long after midnight when he inveigled her out into the garden, on the pretext that she needed rest and cool air; and she saw that his evening's success had excited and stimulated him. He was still young enough to glow with pleasure when he was admired.

He stood under the eucalyptus-scented tree with its canopy of white perfumed flowers, and said, 'Emma, you're magic. I see now why brother Nick desires you.'

Flushed and triumphant, more than a little heady from the wine he had drunk, he reached out for her, and his reaction when Emma dodged was almost comical.

'You want me——' His voice was incredulous. 'Emma, you really do. We're perfect partners—you have to admit that.'

Perfect partners . . . Emma heard that phrase for the second time that evening. She twisted away as Carne reached out to imprison her against the trunk of the flowering gumtree with his arms. She wasn't afraid of him, but she was disinclined for what she now saw Carne believed the logical end to the evening.

He was laughing at her, flushed and triumphant, as she squirmed her way out of his reach. Then Simon's voice said coolly, 'So here you are!'

Emma had never seen anger like the flash that convulsed Carne's face, but he recovered quickly. He stood politely while Simon collected Emma and escorted her indoors to say goodnight to her hosts.

They walked along the breezeway to the door of her small bedroom, next to Simon's. At the doorway he paused.

'Well, Emma, it's been a night of experiences, hasn't it?'

She stared at him solemnly.

'Who would have thought my modest Emma would turn out to be queen of the dance?'

'You didn't invite me to dance.'

'No.' He placed a crooked finger under her chin and lifted her face so that it glowed flower-like in the faint light. 'You made a charming pair, you and the boy. I thought I wouldn't interrupt. And I had—I still have—some talking to do.'

She wouldn't let him know she'd noticed how closely he'd been attending Carolyn. She volunteered lightly, 'You've had a busy evening, I imagine.'

'Yes. I had a few people to talk to. I did warn you, didn't I, before we came.' He bent and kissed her chastely on the forehead.

'That's an enchanting dress, Emma.'

Emma kept her tone flippant.

'You did tell me. Once.'

'I see Carne thought so, too.'

'Just as well somebody did.'

He made a troubled sound then, as though it occurred to him that Emma might have felt neglected. He added, 'Emma, a man has to decide what he wants, and go after it, before it's too late.'

'And you've decided?'

He said grimly, 'What I want right now is to clear my name, to brush the dirt off it. You can understand that, can't you? Trouble is, I don't know where to look next. Young Neville has dodged me all night. I don't want to spoil his celebration. Maybe it's old Foss I should be chasing before he gets too far away.'

He reached out swiftly and curved his two strong hands around her face.

'Carne took care of you, didn't he? Was that a kiss I interrupted in the garden?'

'What do you care?'

Strong fingers remained pressing firmly along her jawline. 'We're engaged, Emma. Remember?' His smile was without warmth. 'You have a commitment to me, for a while longer. After that, if you want to start being choosey——' He sighed then. 'If it's Carne you want——' he began; and without finishing the sentence leaned his head down so that she was aware of his breath feathering her lips.

He said half-humorously, 'Sorry I spoilt your party kiss, Emma,' and took both hands from her face and pinned her with hands and body, against the closed door, holding her immobile while his mouth found hers. He pressed so fiercely against her that his body movements were transmitted through the fragile chiffon as though she were not clothed at all.

When he released her mouth she made a sound of protest, and his lips came back again, this time smiling. He knew what he was doing; sliding the palms of his hands in slow persuasion over her waist and hips and breast, so that when he eventually released her she did not pull away from him angrily but stared at him bemused. Jungle eyes, he had ... glowing, hot and sensual ... amorous mouth curved in a satisfied smile.

He whispered, 'Compensation, Emma,' then he slid one hand behind her and opened the door and gently, ever so gently, guided her inside.

The door clicked shut and she heard his footsteps disappear along the breezeway. He wasn't going to bed. He still had his 'work to do'. But he was packing her away. Had he been jealous of Carne? Never, said Emma's common sense. She was honest enough to realise Carne only wanted her because he believed his big brother had desired her first.

Emma stood inside her room, listening to the irregular beating of her own heart. Compensation, Simon had whispered. Compensation for what? For her, because he'd interrupted Carne's light-hearted attempt at a 'party pass'. Compensation for himself because Carolyn—the 'Caro' of his dreams—had floated so enticingly and disruptively back into his life again, stirring up remembered sensations?

Emma kicked off her shoes and rubbed her ankles. She sat on the bed, aware that she listened for Simon's returning footsteps ... willing him to come back.

Because everything was different now. He would never again be simply Simon Charles, the intimidating man who had rescued her from the driftwood beach. Now he was a mixture of many things: lean brown hands that stirred, muscular body capable of arousing indescribable sensations by coming close to her, the soft mouth that spoke of pleasure without saying words.

From now on, if she were not very careful, every movement he made would intrude upon her senses. So she would have to discipline herself. She supposed she'd calm down soon enough. She certainly didn't want to become emotionally involved with a man as complex and vengeful as this moody, bedevilled companion.

Yet at this moment, if he should come striding back along the breezeway and turn the handle of her door, she would sit like she was sitting now, waiting for the feel of his arms, the touch of his fingers . . .

But there were no footfalls.

'You idiot,' she told herself. 'Do you really imagine kissing you is all that magnificent an experience that he can't wait to come back for more? A man like that, he can get what he wants wherever he wants it.'

She slid off the bed, took off the pearl earrings and the ring, and dropped them gently on the bedside table. Her reflection, blurred because she had only the bedside lamp glowing, showed her the young, young face of an untried girl . . . soft brown-gold hair undisciplined, for all her brushing . . . eyes large and wondering; mouth warm and swollen from Simon's kissing.

She stared at her reflection wryly, then took off the slender white dress, gathered up her night things and got ready for bed.

She wished she could have heard Simon in his bedroom, but the bathroom lay between. She had not even the sounds of occupancy to reassure her. He must still be in the ballroom, dancing . . . or in the garden . . .

Emma pressed her head into the pillow, to shut out the world.

CHAPTER TEN

NEXT morning, Simon let the dawn into Emma's room. He strode in and pulled back the curtains, and when she blinked he said, 'Emma, we're going riding. Do you want to come?'

'Horses? No, thank you. I'd only fall off.'

He laughed. For the first time, she heard his rich, deep laughter.

'Do you mind if I go? Or do you need my company?'

He wore denim jeans and a checked shirt, and under it she saw the gold chain and the diving tern. At least he hadn't discarded that.

She shrugged, 'Go without me. I'll be all right.'

'There's some breakfast in the kitchen. Carry it out to the verandah if you feel like it.'

'I'll do that.'

Seconds later she stood at her window, watching him lope towards the stables. Carolyn waited for him. Of course. Emma saw the sleek bell of blonde hair shining. Carolyn, a perfect figure in light riding clothes. She was beautifully garbed.

Whatever for? Emma asked herself; but she knew the answer. Carolyn intended to catch Simon before he got away a second time, and if looking good would help, then she'd attract his approving eye whenever she possibly could.

Crossly, Emma pulled on her flowered skirt and

rose-coloured top; perversely she walked barefoot on to the verandah, carrying her tray of breakfast.

As she marched outside Carne uncurled himself from a lounger. Emma raised her eyebrows.

'Why aren't you riding?'

He pulled a wry face.

'You know how it is—three's a crowd. Neither of them pressured me, so I didn't force myself on them.'

'Oh.'

So there were just the two of them, Simon and Carolyn. A pair of poised and beautiful people riding in the morning sun. No; they wouldn't pressure Carne to go with them, those two people renewing old acquaintance.

Emma studied Carne covertly, knowing how thin the skin of confidence he wore, how easily he could be stung or discouraged by hearing his brother praised.

She found herself wondering again, could it have been Carne who took his brother's car for a stolen joyride and then left him to pay the price for a moment's inattention?

Carne grumbled bitterly, 'I wonder whose job he'll want, mine or Uncle Doug's. Or will he settle for being boss of Duelgumbah? If he's been among wineries, it could be the vineyards he wants. No wonder dear Uncle Doug is looking so perturbed.'

Then he said contritely, 'You think I'm terrible, don't you? Because I'm honest. It's always worried Doug that Nick would come back eventually and take the whole caboodle away, not to mention discovering old Doug's many errors in management. He's not the world's greatest manager, you know—even I can see that. And Nick would find out quick-smart. Very unsentimental, is brother Nicholas. You measure up, or get out.'

He gave her a crooked grin. 'One thing's certain, your mate Len doesn't have to worry. Nick's not going to settle for anything as humble as public relations.'

'Len's job is important,' Emma pointed out.

'Ah, but it's not the top. Not nearly big enough for Nick. He'll be after the top job, and Grandfather will back him, so he'll get what he wants. If Carolyn has anything to do with it he'll have the lot, and she'll have him.'

He gave Emma an apologetic glance, as she sat with breakfast untasted.

'Sorry, I shouldn't have said that.' Carne grinned. 'You're still in the running, aren't you? Or don't you care?' He smiled at her disarmingly. 'Forget it. I've fallen into a hole, and you'll have to help me climb out. Hurry up with breakfast and I'll show you around the gardens.' He smiled wickedly. 'Much less dangerous in morning light!' His green Delrayo eyes held the flicker of teasing that sometimes showed in Simon's. 'You'll feel a lot safer this morning.'

Duelgumbah and its grounds were very quiet until lunchtime, almost deserted. Most of the guests appeared to be catching up on lost sleep. They drifted out on to the verandah for drinks shortly before noon.

Leitha and her father appeared as Simon and

Carolyn arrived back from their ride. It had been a long ride, Emma thought. A very long ride.

Simon walked on to the verandah and Emma saw that he counted them all, watching keenly to see who was there and who was not.

'Neville not up yet?'

There was a moment's silence, then Leitha put down her drink with a sharp sound on the bar.

'Neville isn't here. He's gone.'

'Where?'

'To Sydney. There was some business Dad wanted him to do.'

'And when will he be back?'

Douglas Delrayo took a long deep swallow from his glass, and his voice was flurried.

'We don't know. A few days, probably. It's—just something I had for him to do. Something urgent. Why?'

'I want to see him.'

Leitha interrupted acidly, 'Well, you can't, can you?' but when Simon turned sharply to look at her some of the bravado vanished and her mouth was sullen.

Douglas Delrayo twisted the glass in his hand. He said, 'It's the old business, isn't it, Nick? You're going to stir it all up again.'

Simon stared at him levelly.

'Wouldn't you?'

Irene Delrayo spoke then. She had come quietly on to the verandah and she had not lost her confidence, but there was an undertone in her voice that could have been pleading.

'Nicholas, it's over. What good can you do?'

Simon's eyes were flint-hard and ruthless. He said harshly, 'I intend to drag out the truth if I have to dig for ever. It should have been done before this.'

'Can't you leave it, Nick? For the family's sake.' Emma saw that Douglas Delrayo trembled. 'It's over, forgotten. None of us holds it against you.'

'It's not over for me. I'll wait for Neville. I'll wait as long as I have to. If I don't find him here, then somewhere else will do. And I'll find Foss——'

'You've been exonerated.'

'Exonerated!' Emma flinched at the lash of Simon's anger. 'Whitewashed, you mean. That's what the whole town thinks; that I got off because I had a good lawyer. And even then it took him all his time, thanks to Neville.'

'You could think of the family. Leave it alone, Nick. For all of us.'

Simon turned on his heel to stride into the house. Emma called his name. 'Simon!' but he did not hear.

Carolyn darted after him, pleading huskily, 'Nicholas! I need a drink,' and he made an angry movement, then took control, and allowed her to entwine her arm with his and lead him to the bar.

Carolyn stared at Emma once, across Simon's bent shoulder as he poured her drink, in a thinly-veiled flash of triumph. Emma put down her glass and walked inside.

As easily as that, he had forgotten the name he

had given her. No wonder Carolyn looked so pleased with herself!

It was early afternoon when Simon found Emma sitting in her favourite position under the trees in the garden, watching the swans on Duelgumbah's small lake.

'Why are you hiding here?' he asked. 'I looked everywhere.'

'Did you?'

She looked up at him wearily. 'I don't know why you bother, she thought. You don't have to be polite any more.

He was frowning now, standing over her, jerking his head impatiently.

'Get up, for heaven's sake. Go and get your hat. I promised to show you the caves behind the waterfall, and now's as good a time as any.'

'You don't have to——'

Emma hid the misery in her eyes behind lowered lashes, and when he pulled her to her feet she demanded tensely, 'Haven't you got better things to do?'

'No, I haven't. Go and get your walking shoes on, and your hat. Plus a long-sleeved shirt. The sun is getting hotter out there.'

As they drove over the dry earth with its dust and scanty trees, Emma was thankful Simon had made her wear the long-sleeved shirt. The heat was hazy and oppressive, her skin pricked by the sun; and when at last they pulled up beside the waterfall her head ached.

When Simon collected a torch from the Land

Rover Emma watched, astonished. It was inconceivable that there should be darkness anywhere in all the landscape. But once behind the waterfall and into the caves, she found herself in a shadowy world. This was not just one cave; it was a labyrinth, linked by small passages and ledges. Simon explained that Aborigines had collected red and yellow ochre from the outer cave for wall paintings and body decoration for rituals.

In the third cave, he flashed the torch over wall-paintings.

'The eel,' he told Emma; and she looked at the creature respectfully.

'No wings.' She couldn't help feeling mildly disappointed.

'No. They were hidden, unfurled only in times of extreme anger or frustration. That's why the elders kept him pacified; and that's why he's painted only with regulation fins. Nicely decorated, though; much more colourful than your ordinary eel.'

'I don't know.' Emma averted her eyes from the snake-like picture. 'He makes me feel nervous.'

She wondered how much Simon had embroidered the legend of the eel. He was quite capable of it; it would amuse him to see her reaction to his dramatic version.

But there certainly had been an eel: his yellow, black and orange presence on the wall of the cave could not be disputed.

At the entrance to the next cave Simon paused. 'Sure you want to go on?'

'Yes, a little farther. I'll never come back here,

it's far too spooky, so I might as well see everything I can. Just don't go too far ahead of me, please.'

Emma shuffled after Simon and the flickering torchlight with decreasing confidence.

'No medicine man on the wall?'

She tried to make it light. They had left the rushing waterfall sound behind them, and there was only the occasional drip, drip of some small spring trickling from the roof.

'No. He's stuck in the waterfall. Move slowly here, the ledge narrows. We aren't going much farther, because there's a deep sinkhole down below, and I don't want to lose you to some subterranean monster.'

Emma said, and to her horror her voice was not quite steady, 'It looks a long way down there, doesn't it?'

All she could see was a seemingly endless number of eroded rock shapes and far below, at the bottom of the cave, the sheen of water, dark and still and far away, in the flickering torchlight.

'How deep is it?' she asked.

'Nobody knows.'

'Can we go now, Simon?'

'Yes. It's time, I think.' His voice sounded concerned. He asked 'Nervous?' as though that were the last thing he had expected of her. Then he added gently, 'They do have an atmosphere, these Aboriginal sacred places. But we haven't disturbed anything, so I don't think the eel will take revenge on us.'

They were turning slowly, carefully, on the ledge when the clattering of falling pebbles came from an outside cave. Simon stiffened, steadied Emma with one hand, and doused the light. There were shuffling footsteps. Emma found herself listening desperately.

She didn't give the eel a passing thought, not the eel with wings nor any other mysterious creature. This was human; the eerie acoustics of the cave picked up the sound of human breathing. Emma heard the hollow plop of another rock on the water below. Simon pushed her into a crevice behind him, and when he was quite sure of her safety he switched off the torch again. But across the darkness of the cave another beam of light, stronger than Simon's, swept over jumbled rockface, down on to the dark skin of the water . . . up again to the sloping roof . . .

'Nick! I know you're in here.'

'Leitha! What the hell are you doing here?'

'I came after you. You knew I would, didn't you? Why couldn't you stay away?'

He said levelly, 'Because this is where I belong, Leitha. This is my home. And I mean to stay here—with a good clean name.'

They heard her sob in the eerie darkness.

'You're a stirrer, aren't you? You had to come and rake it all up again. You were so wild. You did a lot worse things than that accident. You didn't have to come back and send me to prison.'

Stealthily, Simon moved away from Emma, edging along the narrow ledge of jutting rock. He said, 'It was you, Leitha? But you were only a child.'

'Well, I'm not a child now.'

Unexpectedly, Simon's torch stabbed the shadows; Emma saw the glint of a rifle barrel, and her heart thundered in her ears.

She heard the short sharp intake of Simon's breath, then he snapped off the torch. But Leitha knew where they were now; the strong wide beam found them, and settled. Simon edged even farther away from Emma, and the flashlight followed.

'What are doing with that gun, you idiotic girl?'

'There's only one thing to do with it, isn't there? I'm going to get rid of you, leave you in the water. I'll move your Land Rover somewhere else.'

Simon said reasonably, 'Emma had nothing to do with this, leave her alone.'

'It won't work, Nick. I've got a life to live, too. I'm entitled——' Leitha drew a half-sobbing ragged breath. 'You shouldn't have come back to take everything away. You had no right!'

'And what rights do you have, you young monster?'

She cried wildly, 'I was only fourteen. All I wanted to do was drive your car. I didn't plan to hurt anybody. Nev and I went to the Winery in his car and we saw yours and I thought: Now's my chance . . . I made Nev change cars and let me drive. Just a quick flip into town and back while you were busy down by the river.'

'Neville should have known better. A kid your age——'

'I was a good driver. I could handle Nev's car. I often did.'

'And you say *I* was wild!'

'Your Porsche was too powerful for me—that's all it was. And that man came shoving out in his wheelchair from behind a parked bus . . . he was drunk . . . he was always drunk that time of night.'

'And now he's dead. Leitha, put the rifle away, for God's sake,' ordered Simon.

'Don't waste your time trying to talk me out of it! I have to shoot you, and it's your own fault. The two of you——'

She was propping the flashlight against a rock when another voice spoke from the darkness.

'The three of us, Leitha. You'll have to get rid of me, too, daughter.'

'Dad!'

It seemed to Emma that Leitha must surely fall, then. She heard the rush of tiny pebbles as one foot slipped, the watery sound as they landed in the sinkhole. Then Leitha regained her balance, picked up the flashlight, and shone it on the figure of her father outlined against the entrance. When he spoke his voice was jaded and weary. He said, 'It's the end, lass. I can't go any further for you. Blackmail—that rotten leech of an old man—I've bled the Winery, falsified books——' His voice was a weary sound of protest. 'I've turned myself into a liar and a thief for you, Leitha. Because you're my daughter. But not murder——'

They heard her breathing, ragged and fast in the darkness.

'I'll put you down there, too, under the water where nobody will find you. Why did you follow me?'

'I saw you riding after Nick's Land Rover; and I

rode after you. Because today it's all going to stop.'

'I didn't know you were being blackmailed,' Leitha said.

'No. But you did know you persuaded Neville to give false evidence.'

'I had to protect myself.'

Although she could not see him, Emma imagined the distraught man clenching and unclenching his fists as he had that day at the winery.

'Then start with me,' he said. 'Because if you don't, I'll talk.'

'I will. I will if you make me!'

Simon moved in the darkness, as though he fumbled for a closer footing. Leitha impaled him in the beam of light.

'Don't do anything reckless, Nick. I'll shoot your girl-friend before you get here.'

Behind the flashlight Emma thought she saw the faint glimmer of the rifle barrel . . . She heard the click of the safety catch released. She was wondering how terrible the firing of a gun would sound in a small dark cave, when Leitha began to cry.

'I can't—I can't—Oh God, I wish I could die! Why can't I kill myself?'

The gun fell with a clatter, and the flashlight after it, bouncing down like a falling sun until it hit the water.

In the light from Simon's torch Emma saw Leitha crouched on a ledge, her shaking body sagged against the cave wall, face buried in her hands. Then the sobbing ceased.

Douglas's voice sent shock waves through the blackness.

'I'm coming around, Leitha. Don't move.' Then he called to Simon, 'Nick, come with me. We'll take her back. It's safe now.'

'No!'

Emma reached for Simon with her hands ... with her voice ... As she leaned, the outside edge of the rock crumbled, so that she lost balance, and having lost balance she fell before she could stop herself. Instead of touching Simon in the darkness her hands made no contact with anything. She fell, clutching at nothing. As she tumbled she heard Simon shout her name:

'Emma ...!'

He only called it once but it was loud and clear. It sent sound-waves flying and flapping through all the labyrinths of the caves and their passages. It seemed to Emma that as she fell every rock and crevice took up the ragged sound and bounced it back to her.

'Emma ... Emma!'

She felt jutting rock tear at her grasping fingers; and curved them frantically to hold. She heard the sharp crack of breaking stone, hot stabbing on the palms of her hands as sharp edges tore away skin and flesh. She felt the pearl ring wrenched from her finger, and the warm trickle of blood.

Frantically she grasped as she tumbled, breaking her fall but never halting it. 'The black hole', her mind said, because it seemed to be functioning clearly. 'Who would have thought it would be down, instead of up?' All this time the black hole had waited for her. She went down grabbing and scrabbling . . . tearing and bleeding. And overhead she could still hear the crackle of her name being bandied about by the rocks, like a bevy of old women hissing and whispering . . .

'Emma . . . Emma . . .'

CHAPTER ELEVEN

IRENE DELRAYO had once been beautiful. Years and experience had erased the velvet bloom, leaving skin of cobwebbed fragility, eyes of surface brightness hiding pools of reflective sadness. But her hair shone like new silver and her head had the lift of pride, and not a little hauteur, and the strong bones of her face had not lost their arresting quality.

Her mind was sharp as it had ever been and she had dignity because she had never been conquered; and it all showed in her face as she sat, straight-backed and calm, waiting for Emma to open her eyes.

She sat in a hospital chair, weaving a scarf in soft white wool. A young nurse stood beside her, offering coffee and biscuits, but Irene smiled and waved her away. She went back to her secret thoughts.

This was the face that Emma saw when she pushed heavy eyelids against the mists of unconsciousness, and slowly opened her eyes. Nothing else. Not the white hospital walls and the chrome bed, nor the fan whirring in the ceiling. Only the face, with its patient blue eyes and air of dignified waiting.

Emma pushed her tongue against dry lips and tried to shape words.

'Don't talk, my dear.' Irene stood with surprising

speed and grace. 'You're in hospital. You had a fall, but you'll soon be all right. Just a little time.'

Emma remembered—the fall, and Simon's calling. Shadows whirling as Leitha's flashlight dropped.

She hadn't drowned in the sinkhole, then. Her fall must have been broken. Her head ached with innumerable throbbings. She tried to lift her hands, but they were heavy with bandages. Pain shot the complete length of her arms and exploded in her head, blotting out reality.

The next time Emma opened her eyes it wasn't quite so difficult. She was stronger. She kept her eyelids open and studied the fine profile of Irene Delrayo, who watched something outside the window.

Irene turned her head and seeing Emma awake she smiled, and Emma's heart lurched, because this was Simon's smile. For all his strong resemblance to his grandfather, Simon smiled his grandmother's smile.

Nicholas, Emma reminded herself sadly. Not Simon. He was Nicholas now. She would have to remember that, and it would take some remembering.

She sighed, and Irene beckoned the nurse. Emma let them fuss over her. Back at Duelgumbah she had developed the desolate sensation of being alone. Nobody needed her. Her role as Simon's 'camouflage' was over. She had nobody to cook for, argue with, or listen to, even to care for.

She'd hated the feeling. Recollection of it turned her weakness to tears; she was horrified to feel them squeeze out from under closed eyelids and trickle down her cheeks. Her bandaged hands refused to lift and brush them away.

Soft fingers touched Emma's cheeks. 'That's good.' It was Irene Delrayo's voice whispering. 'That's very good.'

'Good?'

The old lady nodded.

'To wash away the bitterness,' she said. 'Sometimes I wish men could cry. You might wish that yourself some day, if you have sons.'

Once more Emma remembered Simon—Nick, she corrected herself—calling out of his nightmares; and in a flash of comprehension she knew that his grandmother understood all of that and how he must have felt. Emma thought, five years. Nearly six years, of exile for a loved grandson because you had to consider first the welfare of the man you married. I hope I never have to make that kind of decision.

In a surge of pity she moved her face gently against the ministering hand. Irene let it rest there a few moments.

'Now, Emma, we've to get you out of bed and into the world again.'

Emma nodded weakly.

Once she had taken the first steps, it wasn't so very difficult. She'd been unconscious for several days; her balance was affected and she was pleased Simon wasn't there to see her tottering from bed to chair, and stumbling back again.

Irene explained that he and Douglas had gone together searching for old Foss.

'That dreadful man,' she agonised. 'That horrible creature! All those years blackmailing!'

'Your husband—Simon's—I mean Nick's grandfather—doesn't he need you?'

'He's all right, better than he's been for years. It's such a relief to finally know what happened. Philip is distressed about Douglas, of course, and appalled by that silly little Leitha. Poor Douglas,' she mourned, 'making such foolish decisions.'

'He knew all the time?' queried Emma.

'No. Not until everything was long over and Nicholas had gone abroad. Then Foss presented himself with his first demand. It must have been a terrible shock. He suffered, poor Douglas, but that doesn't excuse what he did to Nick.'

So Simon was searching for Foss. He would not be visiting the hospital. Emma said painfully, 'Mrs Delrayo, please don't stay here on my account. I'm getting stronger every day. I'm sure you ought to be with your husband.'

'He ordered me to stay with you. They both did—he and Nicholas.' She laughed tremulously. 'Two men to bully me about! I'd better obey.'

The days that strengthened Emma lifted some of the sadness from Irene Delrayo. She laughed often, telling Emma stories of family history that put things together for Emma as nothing else could have done. Talking about her grandson, calling him Nick or Nicholas, never Simon.

So that each day Emma found the Simon Charles she knew turning into the rich pampered grandson who hadn't hesitated to choose a scarlet Porsche for his birthday, who had visited Europe on holidays, who had been equipped from birth to handle life with supreme confidence, then had it all fall apart one crucial evening.

Irene Delrayo had pain in her eyes when she talked about today's Nicholas.

'I expect you find what I did unforgivable,' she suggested. 'It was like deserting Nicholas, when he needed us most. Yet I had to do it. The doctor warned me. People thought him guilty, and people can be so cruel. The doctors warned that the least stress might kill Philip. There was so much unpleasantness for a while. We had letters . . . accusations . . . unpopularity in the town. It was such a terrible thing to happen . . . that poor man!'

'It must have been difficult for you,' commented Emma.

Irene showed a flash of the old proud woman. 'I can deal with unpleasantness, and so could my husband before his illness. But after that, his strength was gone. He became emotionally distressed so easily. Little things upset him terribly. He grieved over them. So what could I do?'

She looked at Emma wistfully.

'You're sure you wouldn't have done that—kept a young man away from everything and everybody he loved?'

Emma shook her head.

'I don't know. I really don't know.'

Carne arrived next morning. He announced, 'Big brother contacted the homestead and left orders for me to come and see how the invalid is progressing.'

His arrival caused a stir among the nurses. Emma watched with amusement the surreptitious sprucing-up, the bright-eyed interest, as Carne entered the wards.

She didn't blame them. Tall and elegant and by far the handsomest young man she, or they, would probably ever see, he brought her magazines, he made her laugh; he talked sweet-talk.

He walked with her in the hospital grounds and when she was fit to become an outpatient there were more than a few bright eyes watching enviously as she walked to the waiting car supported by Carne's affectionate arm.

Of course he noticed the attention he aroused; it must have amused him to create such a stir.

Emma spent more time as an outpatient before going back to the homestead. She had sprained one elbow and there were deep cuts on arms and hands, as well as a wound on the back of her neck that required attention.

Simon—Nick—had directed that she stay at a motel, and Irene and Carne stayed with her. Irene got in touch with Duelgumbah several times, but each time reported Simon still away. Foss had collected a large final payment from Douglas the evening after the rodeo, and disappeared. But they would find him.

'Oh yes.' Irene nodded her proud head. 'Nick will find him. He never lets go.'

'I know,' said Emma. Most of the bandages were off her hands and she was sadly conscious of her bare finger, without the pearl ring.

She became used to Carne's goodnatured teasing

as he drove to and from the hospital for her treatment.

'Looking after you isn't such an ordeal, Emma. I feel as if I've been born to it. Why don't you consider me as more than just a friend? I could cherish you. You'd have a wonderful time at Duelgumbah, or the Winery. I can see you flitting about barefoot in your coloured skirts with your hair flying and your tantalising lips. Something to set the sophisticated ladies talking, that would be. How would you like that, Emma? My grandfather would give us a vineyard, or an outstation somewhere if you prefer it. I could make you so happy.'

He really believed it. What big brother Nicholas wanted, Carne wanted too. He pleaded so intensely sometimes. He had no idea how quickly he'd tire of her once he'd coaxed her away from Nick. But Emma knew.

When he talked about his brother, the envy showed so clearly.

'Nick the infallible, we used to call him. He rode harder, ran faster, thought quicker than anyone else. Outdid us all without any trouble. Made a point of it, did brother Nick.'

Emma could imagine that. Of course, he would always be ahead. She looked at Carne, not without sympathy. It must be discouraging, following in the footsteps of a human dynamo, always suffering comparison.

Good-looking though he was, there was weakness in Carne. It showed in the soft mouth; the way he took care to say what pleased; not yet sure enough to be himself.

Emma remembered Simon's nightmare, and shivered. Was that the high cost of self-sufficiency? She wondered whether Simon considered it worth the price.

Emma was discharged from hospital one clear sunny morning when the honey-eaters were making bird-sounds in the trees and a warm wind stirred the dust into spirals along the edge of the road.

'Nick's back,' Carne told her. 'He offered to fly down and collect us, but I told him one of the doctors has to go close to Duelgumbah to look at a stockman. So we may as well fly back with him.'

Emma's disappointment must have shown. Carne added, looking aggrieved, 'If you don't like those arrangements I can get in touch with Nick again.'

But pride demanded that she travel with Irene and Carne; not send for Simon who was now Nick and might not want her.

They arrived at the small airstrip on Duelgumbah earlier than expected. Douglas Delrayo picked them up in his own car.

Philip Delrayo waited on the verandah of the homestead. Emma thought he looked stronger, not so defeated any more.

She told him she was sorry to have kept his wife away for so long, and he said, 'I've been fine, thank you, my dear. Carolyn came to look after me, and there have been others. Nick and Douglas arrived home yesterday, so we are all here together at last.'

Yes, Emma agreed silently. They were all here together. The Delrayo family and Carolyn and the grandson who had been lost.

Simon and Carolyn had been riding. They rode their horses along the driveway, and Emma saw the caravan parked under a stand of golden cypress trees.

When they came close—very close—Emma saw with a bitter sense of shock that Simon had shaved off his beard. Now he was indeed a stranger.

Philip Delrayo wheeled his chair close to where Emma sat.

'How do you like Nicholas cleanshaven? It's a great improvement, isn't it?'

'Yes,' Emma lied, 'a great improvement.' And looking at the man on the black stallion, she knew what she had known before, but had tried desperately not to bring with her from the hospital: that Simon Charles had disappeared for ever. Not dramatically, in a great puff of smoke like a magician's trick, but slowly, inevitably, during the weeks she had been away, Simon Charles had been absorbed into the bright and splendid man who was now Nicholas Delrayo.

She had considered Carne handsome, but he was only a pale reflection of the powerful man who tossed the reins to a stablehand and walked to the verandah.

Simon Charles hadn't even paused to look back. Not once in all those three weeks had he appeared at her bedside with a look, a touch, to reassure her. Perhaps he had been too busy collecting reassurance for himself, after all the bitter years.

Certainly, in the splendid man approaching there seemed no trace of the bitterness and anger that had haunted Simon Charles. So she should be glad for him.

He came and stood beside her and Emma tilted her face so that her eyes met his calmly, even casually.

He said, 'Emma!' and bent to kiss her cheek. She tilted her head back farther.

'I'd forgotten how tall you are.' Despite the aching in her heart she managed to keep her voice cool and calm.

He said, 'And you? You're looking well, in spite of everything.' His searching eyes must not see her hidden misery. He flicked her cheek lightly. 'I think you might have put on a little weight, Emma. It suits you.'

No wonder Carolyn wanted him. Emma wondered how, even when disaster threatened and scandal, Carolyn could ever have considered choosing anyone else.

Irene Delrayo asked, 'Did you find that horrid old man?'

'We did. He'd gone into hiding in Sydney, but we tracked him down. We confiscated what money he had left, and frightened the hell out of him. He won't come back to Luradil, and I don't imagine he'll try blackmailing again.'

The doctor stayed to lunch and so did Douglas Delrayo. Carolyn seemed to be a permanent resident.

After lunch Douglas called Emma into the library, and Simon followed.

'I wanted you to know,' Douglas said, 'how sorry I am. Not that it's much use, an apology I mean, but I bitterly regret what happened to you.'

He looked around the booklined room, with its red cedar desk and comfortable chairs, as if he might find in its comfort the right words to say.

'There's all the rest of it, too. What happened to Nicholas—the man in the wheelchair, the theft. All of it so unworthy. Bottom of the barrel, isn't it?'

His haunted eyes turned to Nick, but Nick remained unbending. He said, 'You're lucky Emma isn't dead. I'd have killed you with my bare hands.'

The older man's fingers clutched a chairback. He held it desperately, as though he leaned on it for strength.

Emma spoke impulsively.

'I'm all right. And I don't bear grudges.'

'And you, Nick?' When Nick remained tight-lipped Douglas continued, 'I can't ask you to forget. But you're not the only one to suffer. I've had five years despising myself, losing every shred of self-respect. You can send me to jail, Nick, you and the family. I won't deny anything—misappropriation of funds, just plain theft. You can have a written confession. I don't suppose you'll ever understand, any of you, but hang it all, man, she's my daughter.'

The taut grey face searched Nick's expression for any sign of softening and found none. He said desperately, as though the words were wrung out of him, 'Suppose it had been Emma?'

And Simon stood arrested, staring at him haughtily across the polished desk.

Emma turned and quietly left the room.

'Suppose it had been Emma' . . . now there's a laugh. She walked along the breezeway to her room and her knees were shaking. Not for a scrawny little beach girl would the great Nicholas Delrayo stoop to dirty his hands in double-dealing. Not for anybody, if it came to that.

Emma was searching for her hat in her bedroom when Simon knocked at the door. He said, 'Emma, I've something important to do this afternoon. Will you be all right till I come back?'

'Yes, I'm perfectly all right.'

He had changed into denims and Emma saw with pain that he no longer wore the golden tern under his shirt. The strong lean face was enigmatic, the deep, deep green eyes kept their secrets.

'We'll talk when I come back. We have a lot of talking to do.'

He took three long strides into the room and cupped her face in his hands. His smile nearly tore her apart.

'Well, Emma, you may be flitting around your own vineyard yet.'

She jerked away from him. So he thought like the rest of them, like Carolyn and Leitha. Like Carne. Carne had been amused. 'I can see you flitting about in your long coloured skirts . . . something to set the sophisticated ladies talking . . .'

She forced her voice to remain calm.

'I don't need you to tell me,' she answered him clearly, 'that I don't belong here. I'd never fit in, would I? I'm no grand lady. I wouldn't want to be.'

He swung around in surprise.

'Emma! That's not what I meant.'

He said no more, because Douglas Delrayo called along the breezeway and Carolyn came after him.

Emma heard Simon's voice say softly, 'Oh damn!' Then—'See you later, Emma.' Then he was gone.

Carolyn had changed before lunch into a blue cotton dress with tiny shoulderstraps, that flattered her figure. She could have decorated the pages of a fashion magazine instead of the breezeway of a cattle station.

She stood in Emma's doorway, in the place where Simon had left, coolly watching Emma arrange her hat.

She queried calmly, 'Planning to stay long?' Emma stared at her numbly. Carolyn's scornful eyes assessed everything that Emma wore, the flowered skirt, the casual top. 'You could make things very unpleasant for Nick. Is that what you're planning? Playing poor little invalid, making sure he feels guilty. Why don't you let him go? You know you'll have to, in the end.'

'I'm not playing invalid!'

'He's too big a man to send you away yet. But I'll tell you: whatever you had going with Nick—if there ever was anything—your poor little liaison is over. Well and truly finished. Nick's back where he belongs. And no matter how you hang on, the outcome's going to be the same, isn't it? There's no future in it for you, Emma. This isn't your kind of world.'

'I've no intention of hanging on.' Emma forced the words through stiff lips. 'I'm leaving as soon as I can.'

Carolyn studied her insolently.

'Why not today?' Seeing Emma's confusion she pressed further. 'The doctor is flying over to the coast this afternoon. He could drop you there. You might wait weeks before you get another chance.' She inspected Emma calmly, cruelly. 'That's where you belong, isn't it? On the beach somewhere. Nick says you have friends up north. Why don't you join them? It's better than hanging around here until you're pushed out. And believe me, you'll be asked to go eventually.'

'Yes,' Emma's lips puckered in a crooked smile, 'I suppose it is.'

'You'll go, then, with the doctor?'

It was Carolyn who organised Emma a seat in the plane, Carolyn who whisked her out to the airstrip when time for take-off arrived. There was no one moving around the homestead. They were all out, or resting or sleeping.

Carolyn had offered, 'If you need money I'm sure something can be arranged,' but Emma found the door of the caravan unlocked. She took whatever money remained in the drawer. She packed a few of the clothes Simon had bought her—jeans, the parka, the yellow shirt and the shirt she'd worn to bed the night of Simon's nightmare.

'You'd better tell the pilot where you want to go,' Carolyn instructed coldly. 'As far north as he can, I expect.'

Emma shook her head.

'The Sapphire Coast will do. There's a beach I want to—to v-visit—before I join my brother and his friends.'

When the plane took off, a cloud of dust funnelled up and blotted out the view, and Emma was glad. She didn't want to look back at Duelgumbah.

Nor would she look down at the green valley of Luradil if they passed over it, with its trees and flowers and green vines beside the shining river.

CHAPTER TWELVE

IN Jerinda, Emma booked herself a seat on the coach travelling north next morning. She left her small bundle of clothing at the tourist office and walked along the clifftops until she came to the driftwood beach.

It was crowded with surfers this afternoon; boys and girls in rubber wetsuits launching themselves on to the green water; rescuing their boards from the white choppy swirl inshore; or running along the sand with precious surfboards under their arms.

Emma sat on a bench at one of the picnic tables and watched the beach below. Later, when everyone had gone, she lowered herself on to the grass and sat hunched forward, hugging her knees, listening to the surf-sounds.

The dusk came down, and then the dark. Shapes blurred, a few stars pricked the sky. Emma spared a small, painful thought for the little Aboriginal girl whose tear-stained eyes might be among them.

Who needed a black hole in the sky? She knew she would carry her own emptiness with her from now on; the dark hole that had once held the shape and the nearness of Simon Charles, who no longer needed her.

The night was warm, and Emma planned to sleep in a fold in the dunes later. She was not nervous. Even when footsteps sounded behind her she turned slowly and without much curiosity to see who was approaching.

A lopsided moon pushed straggling beams of light through the banksia trees, but Emma did not need the light to know that it was Simon striding towards her out of the trees.

Oh, but he was angry! She sensed his anger in the deliberate way he walked, taking those giant strides across the grass. But when he saw her face he checked and slowly, silently, lowered himself on to the ground beside her.

Emma studied him gravely.

'You didn't have to come chasing after me.'

'Who did you want? Carne?'

'No. Carne is a nice boy, but he's too young for me.'

The moonlight made white marble of her skin and her eyes were dark and solemn.

'How did you find me?' she asked.

'I shook Carolyn until her bones rattled. She told me you mentioned something about a beach you wanted to see before you joined your brother. I hoped it was this place. I couldn't think of any other.'

He was very careful not to touch her, although he sat so close she could detect the rise and fall of his breathing.

He said, 'Emma, tell me something. The age difference between us, do you find it—appalling?'

She knew by the timbre of his voice, the way he tried to keep it light, as though he asked a trivial thing, that the question was important, and she must think carefully about her answer. If she said the wrong thing he'd leave, believing she didn't care for him. But if she was wrong, and he really didn't want her as much as she hoped, then she could embarrass him.

She licked dry lips and swallowed and said in a low voice, 'I don't find anything about you appalling.'

So if she was wrong and he didn't love her, that left him a way out. He didn't have to take it any further. But when she heard the long escaping breath, as though some great tension had been released, she knew she had been right. She turned her head, so that her mouth was close to his, and smiled.

'I thought you knew,' she said.

He delved in his short pocket and held out one hand. On the brown palm lay her pearl ring, gleaming in the dimness.

'How could you find it? It was lost in the cave.'

'We went back this afternoon, Douglas and two of the stockmen and myself, with ropes and spotlights. And we found it. Luckily it was wedged in a crevice. If it had fallen into the sinkhole I'm afraid that would have been the end of it. We'd have had to buy you another.'

He smiled then, the piercing sweet Delrayo smile that started ripples of response somewhere deep in her body.

'This is the original, Emma. Our engagement ring.' He put the ring on her finger, then he reached out one hand and Emma felt the strong fingers curl over hers.

She hated to ask the question, but she knew she must.

'Not the diamond? The Delrayo diamond?'

'That, too,' he promised. 'For extras.'

'*Some* extras!'

'Who told you about the diamond?' he asked.

'Carolyn. That it was hers once.'

He nodded grimly.

'She handed it back to me. Thank God.'

'You were glad?'

'Oh, not when it happened. I thought, another rat—another betrayal.' He touched her hair lightly. 'I wanted to throw it in the river. I'm glad I didn't, if you'll wear it sometimes.' He touched the pearl ring on her finger. 'This is the one that matters. The ring that will marry me to you. You *will* marry me, Emma?'

She nodded blissfully.

'If you want me. I'll be an instant bigamist.'

He lifted his head sharply. 'How come?'

'I'll marry two men at the one time. Simon Charles and Nicholas Delrayo.'

'One man,' he insisted, and his voice was harsh. 'One heart. One love. One pair of hands.'

But he was wrong, and Emma knew it. She was marrying two men. For deep inside the splendid stallion that was Nicholas Delrayo she would always see Simon Charles, who had cried out his pain in the night and turned to her for comfort. He would always be there. Like the pearl in the ring, the moon on the river. She said, 'You don't wear the golden tern any more.'

'I broke a link. It's at the jeweller's, being fixed.'

'Why didn't you come and see me at the hospital?'

'I wanted to. But I thought it only fair you should have a chance to find out if you wanted somebody nearer your own age. I knew Carne was attracted. Those three weeks,' he remembered. 'They were the longest time of my life. Longer than the years abroad.'

'You and Douglas—are you friends again?'

'Yes.' His voice was oddly humble. 'We understand each other now. Do you remember, Douglas said "Suppose it had been Emma!"—and I knew that I would lie for you, and steal for you, and pay black money. Whatever was necessary, I would have done. So I can't sit in judgment on Douglas. He's miserable enough, anyway. He'll take a long time to forgive himself.'

'Did you find out who searched the caravan?'

'Neville. Urged and persuaded by Leitha, of course.'

'What will you do about Leitha?' asked Emma.

'Nothing. It's over. Finished.'

He twisted the fingers of one hand in her hair, pulling her face so that it came close to his own.

'Emma!' His cheek against her cheek. He slid her towards him, supporting her head with one arm, the soft cloud of hair spread over his shoulder. His lips touched her lips, playing with them teasingly until Emma felt featherings of delight stir all over her slender body.

She could not stop herself; she pressed herself against his strength, making small sounds of pleasure in response to his kissing, while the strong arms pulled her even closer.

To her astonishment, she felt a ripple of laughter

shake his shoulders. He lifted his head and let her see his laughing mouth. His face was young and bright. He asked, 'Well, Emma, how is it? So-so?'

He was vibrant with joy and confidence, but Emma's lips were shaking and so was her body. Simon had to bend his head to catch the whisper of her answer.

'Scarey. A little.'

He made a sound of protest, resting his face in the softness of her hair.

'Emma, don't ever be afraid of me.'

And then he gentled her, soft-talking and persuading, while his hands searched under the fragile blouse, smoothing away apprehension. Shoulders and breasts and soft throat responded to his loving, until at last Emma let herself be carried away by the tide of feeling.

She slid her hands under the silk shirt, feeling his body tremble at the contact. So then she knew that for every pleasure he could offer her she would have something to give him in return. She moved her mouth against his, joyfully.

And even then he checked. He took his mouth from her ardent clinging and looked down at her, the green eyes waiting, questioning.

Emma lifted her arms and clasped her fingers together around his body, tilting back her head until she felt the quickening of his breathing.

She lifted her young face, soft and white and eager in the moonlight, pulling his mouth down towards hers so that she might give him, freely and fully, the gift of her love.

Harlequin Plus

WHAT'S A RED HERRING?

In *The Driftwood Beach* Simon calls Emma his "red herring," because her "innocent face is going to disarm suspicion" while he returns to his hometown to conduct a personal investigation into an incident that occurred five years earlier and has greatly affected his life since.

Where did the term "red herring," meaning "camouflage" come from? Well, the answer is really quite simple. One way of curing a herring is to salt it and smoke it slowly over a wood fire. The herring turns a dark reddish brown and becomes strongly flavored and scented—so scented, in fact, that it overwhelms any other smell! In folklore, red herrings were used to throw hounds off a scent; a fish was drawn across the trail, and the hounds would become totally confused.

Writers of mystery stories, too, deliberately misguide readers as to the identity of the guilty party by planting misleading clues and information—and these are known as red herrings.

Simon is quite right to call Emma his red herring, but fortunately for her, by the end of Samantha Harvey's story Simon thinks of Emma as something far more than that!